Stat

Book 2 of Hugh, Vampire

By Robert P. Wills

Any similarities between people living or dead is coincidental. The names of actual planets, moons, or other celestial bodies, as well as businesses thereon are to make the narrative more realistic; no endorsement is implied.

"They should all should taste my blade!"

- Hinata Takahashi

One

Hugh let out a long breath and shook his head. It was overwhelming flying the large space craft. While he was fairly good at flying airplanes, it had always been in clear conditions. It had also been with either an instructor, or on a short trip- to avoid authorities. His first solo flight had been on a clear night and an easy, straight shot from Teller to Nome- just 78 miles. The aircraft he was in was large, but not nearly as large as the spaceship he was currently piloting. He also landed the Grumman Albatross on the wide-open Norton Sound far from any moored boats, then taxied straight toward and onto the rocky beach. There really wasn't anything for him to run into besides the shore. Now he was worried how much maneuvering he would have to do to land the spaceship at an airlock. Running into the side of a building would definitely set off alarms and have authorities show up to ask questions.

Flying to another planet seemed like an absurdly impossible task.

While most of the ship's functions were automated, he still felt the need to monitor them; at least until he felt confident in the onboard computer. He understood what the various readouts the computer showed him were; speed, power levels, temperatures but not much else. He decided he would pilot the ship himself until they were past the Moon. From there he would engage the autopilot. "Man, this whole caring about people is turning out to be a lot of trouble." Hugh let out another long breath.

"Are you okay?" Isaac asked.

Hugh snapped out of his introspection; he had almost forgotten about the young man. "Me? Sure, I'm fine." He shook his head again. "I'm just piloting a space ship to another planet for the first time ever."

Isaac smiled. "You're doing great, Brother Hugh." He looked down at the viewscreen. "The Earth looks so small from here."

"It was a lot smaller before; people used to travel all over it," Hugh said. "It's gotten bigger and slower, which isn't a bad thing."

Isaac just nodded, unsure how to even answer.

The ship arced over the Earth and headed toward the moon. The onboard computer said they would reach it within an hour at the speed they were traveling. "Why don't we get something to eat?" Hugh asked. "We're on a pretty good path to the Moon."

Isaac smiled wide. "I think that's a great idea." He rubbed his stomach. "I've been looking at the kitchen and I'm not sure how it works, but I'm excited to try some of the food."

Hugh tapped the autopilot button then stood. "Then let's get to it." He raised his voice slightly. "Cynthia, alert me if any spacecraft get nearby."

"Quantify nearby." Cynthia replied.

"You don't know what nearby is?" Hugh stopped walking.

"Nearby is a relative term," Cynthia said. "Provide a distance to require an alarm."

Hugh thought for a moment; he had no idea how close was too close for a spacecraft to be. "How close does a ship need to be to contact us?"

"All ships within the solar system are able to contact each other because of relay satellites and buoys, time dilation notwithstanding."

Hugh frowned. "Do ships have scanners where they could see how many people are aboard this ship?"

"Scanners like that are not feasible; they are only in science fiction stories." Cynthia said.

"What can the onboard sensors of a ship determine?"

"Sensors can determine how much energy a particular ship is putting out to extrapolate speed and trajectory. They can read the information from another ship's transponder to learn a ship's ownership and specifications as well as where the ship is registered. They can determine if an atmosphere is breathable. They can…"

"Stop, Cynthia. Stop." Hugh said. He considered what the AI had said. "But our transponder isn't on, right?" Hugh asked. It was one of the first things he did when he first took over the ship.

"Correct."

"How would a ship notice us then?" Hugh asked, almost sorry he had started what seemed to be turning into a long conversation with the ship's AI. He gestured toward the galley. "Go. We can talk on the way."

Isaac nodded then opened the hatch to the rear of the ship. He stepped through then looked back at Hugh expectedly.

"If we are within a hundred thousand miles of another ship, their proximity alerts would let them know we were here." Cynthia explained. "Active navigational sensors are used to avoid uncharted space debris, asteroids, and other ships."

"Even without our transponder being on?"

"Yes. Even without a transponder, a ship produces an electronic signature that would alert a navigational sensor."

"Fine then." Hugh said as he stepped through the hatch. "If we have a ship pass within a hundred thousand miles of us and they are on an intercepting course, alert me." He said, hoping that space would be like the ocean; when a ship saw another ship in the distance, they would just continue on their way.

"Okay, alert parameters set." Cynthia confirmed.

Two

Isaac stood in front of the microwave oven looking at the numbers. "I don't understand how this works."

Hugh laughed. "I don't either, but I know how to use it."

"You don't know how this works?" Isaac looked at him.

"Well, I understand it uses microwaves to cook food by heating up the water within it, but I couldn't take it apart and fix it." Hugh admitted. "Using it is simple. You just pick how long you want something to cook and then hit start. If it's not hot, cook it some more. If it's too hot or burned, cook it less next time."

Isaac smirked. "Trial and error? I thought you understood this technology."

"That might be an overstatement. I could use these ovens from my time well enough but even then there were a lot of things I did not understand but could operate. I can build a canoe; I can't build an engine." Hugh stepped in front of the oven. "But this thing might work faster than what I am used to. So we'll go with what used to work the last time I used one of these; high power for two minutes." He looked at the storage compartment. "What are you in the mood for?"

"What?"

"What sort of food do you want?" Hugh pressed a button on the compartment door which closed an external vent; the storage unit kept food frozen by exposing it to the vacuum of space; it was simple, reliable, and used no energy at all. He pulled the door open. "Let's see." He looked at the square packages inside. "We have beef stew, macaroni, chili, chicken, steak." He smiled. "Have you ever had macaroni?"

"I don't know what that is." Isaac said. "I know what stew is, and the other things as well."

"I'll have the macaroni and you can taste it to see what you think. It's a flour noodle."

"Like spätzle?" Isaac said, referring to a German egg noodle served with various kinds of meats and usually a gravy.

"Kind of. Except longer and it has a tomato sauce on it." Hugh said. "You do the stew." He took two square packages out of the compartment then closed the door. A hissing sound emanated from it as the air was pumped out before the outer vent was opened. He handed the stew package to Isaac.

Isaac tapped the package against the counter. "This is frozen solid. How long will it take that oven to cook this?"

"Two, three minutes, tops. We'll do two then stir it." Hugh opened the oven door. "Yours first." He pointed at the package. "Peal a corner open so that the steam can vent out. And pull that fork and knife off the top"

Isaac pulled a corner of the package open and peered in. There were chunks of meat and vegetables inside with a frozen brown gravy around it all. "How do they make this?" He put the container into the oven.

"Fork and knife." Hugh reminded.

"Oh!" Isaac took the container out again and pulled off what seemed to be pressed cardboard eating utensils. "It's all in one package." He put the container back in the oven. "Neat."

"That way there's less to clean. Storage space was always an issue on ocean going ships. I guess it's the same in space. Three minutes is three, zero, zero." Hugh pressed buttons. "Then hit start." He put his container on the counter and opened a drawer. "They cook the vegetables and meat like you normally would, then they freeze it solid so that it will keep for a very long time. When you are ready to eat it, you just heat it up."

Isaac nodded. "Like we do meat in the winter time. When we don't smoke it."

"Exactly." Hugh took two paper cups from a dispenser and filled them with water. He looked around. "Seems these people have figured out artificial gravity."

"What?"

"The water doesn't float away." He looked down. "And neither do we." He remembered what Baxter had told him: 'It's Oganesson compressed until it reached a singularity.' So, part of the gravitational thrust was used to keep everything and everyone oriented on the ship. He looked at Isaac. "They've figured out how to make gravity on this little ship."

"What?"

"Nothing. It would be too hard to explain."

The pair watched the numbers count down in silence. Hugh was happy that Isaac didn't ask how the counter worked, or how the numbers lit up. LEDs were also something that he was very familiar with but also didn't know how they worked.

Finally, the microwave chimed.

"Oh, here we go." Isaac said. "I am getting hungry."

"You're always hungry." Hugh opened the door and pulled out the steaming container. "See how this tastes." He quickly moved it onto the table. "Careful that's really hot." He put the two waters on the table. "Now let's see how Martians make spaghetti." He put his meal in the oven and turned it on. "I don't have my hopes up."

Isaac picked up a piece of meat and blew on it. After a moment, he put it in his mouth. As he chewed his eyes swiveled to Hugh.

"Good? Bad? What?"

"It doesn't taste like anything." Isaac said as he swallowed. "It's just... there."

"Huh." Hugh turned and opened the cupboard above the sink. There were several containers in them. He opened them and smelled them one after another. Finally, he held one up. "This smells kind of like mesquite." He hesitated. "It's spicy. Try some of this."

Isaac took the container and shook some of it onto his food then smelled it. "Well, it smells better anyway." He smiled. "Maybe I can try one of the other ones since this is a small portion."

Hugh shook his head; the container had what he considered a very large portion of stew in it. "Small portion? If you say so." When the oven chimed, he took his container out and moved to the table. He let Isaac try some of his spaghetti.

"I'm not too sure about Martian food." Isaac said. "It doesn't taste like anything."

Hugh nodded. "I guess they just eat for nutrition. Or maybe Baxter was just cheap when it came to stocking the galley." He noticed Isaac was staring at him as he ate. "What?"

"What?" Repeated Isaac.

"What are you staring at? I can eat food you know. You've seen me do it before."

Isaac looked back at his food. "No, that's not it. It's just…"

"Just what?"

"It's nothing." Isaac said. "I'm going to make a chili next to see how it is." He stood and moved to the cabinet that had the food in it.

"Isaac. If there's something bothering you, you need to let me know. We're going to be stuck in this little ship for the next few days so we really can't have any secrets."

"I was just thinking of something, that's all. But it's nothing."

"Isaac." Hugh pointed his fork at him. "What is it? Am I chewing too loudly? Slurping my spaghetti too much?"

Isaac laughed as he retrieved a chili package. "Two minutes? Three was pretty hot."

"You can try two. Or even two and a half." Suggested Hugh. "Stop changing the subject."

Isaac put his chili in the oven and turned it on. "It's just that you're really smart when it comes to things like this so I don't want to insult you."

Hugh held his hands out. "Things like this? Isaac, this is my very first space ship ever. I'm learning as I go here and this thing terrifies me. If you have something that could be helpful, spit it out."

"I think we should go to Deimos first and we should do it in the morning. Their time in the morning. Like around nine. In the morning."

"Oh. Okay. At least it wasn't my eating." He put his fork down. "So why is that?"

"Oh, I didn't mean to get you upset." Isaac said.

"I'm not upset." Hugh said a little louder than he meant to. "I mean… I'm curious why you think that." He held his hands out. "Because I'm open to suggestions and if you've got a good reason, then let's hear it. Please."

"Well, I tend the animals, you know?"

"I know."

"And I'm there first thing in the morning. Before dawn to milk the cows." Isaac said. "There's twenty-six of them now, you know."

"I did not know that." Hugh admitted. Now worried that the young man was off on one of his famous tangents with no ending in sight.

"And then once I'm done with the cows, I feed the horses." Isaac hesitated. "There's lots of them. Over thirty even."

"Thirty horses, twenty-six cows. Got it." Hugh tried to remain calm.

"Then, after I feed the horses I've got nothing to do until it's time to get the eggs from the chickens which I do about noon."

"I am not even going to guess the number of chickens there are." Hugh said.

"A hundred thirteen." Isaac said. "But that's not the point."

Hugh smiled. "There's a point?"

"Well, between feeding the horses and checking on the chickens, I really have nothing to do so I go back to town."

"Okay." Hugh looked at the timer on the oven- he wondered if Isaac would get to his point before the chili was done. There was a minute left on the timer. "And?" He coaxed.

"And that's about eight thirty, nine o'clock." Isaac said.

"So, it's a lucky time for you? Nine o'clock?"

"No." Isaac said. "When I get back to town, there's no one there. Everyone is out working so I usually either work in the wood shop or go to the library because everyone is away."

"Oh, I get it." Hugh said as realization hit him.

"Right?" Isaac nodded. "And if Deimos is just a place where people live. Where rich people live. That means they work someplace else. Probably on Mars, that means in the day time, they should all be off doing whatever job they have someplace else."

Hugh nodded. "And if we wait until night time, then pretty much everyone will be back by then." He smiled. "That does make sense." He held up a finger. "Except for the help."

"What help?" Issac looked at the microwave as it chimed. "Help with what?"

"The servants." Hugh said.

"Servants? They are servants for people?" Hugh nodded. "Whoever wants to become great among you must be your servant, and whoever wants to be first must be your slave."

"No, they aren't servants in a Biblical sense; they *have* servants. They are people they hire because they're busy with other things. They are people who take care of the house; cleaners, cooks and such."

Isaac took the chili from the oven and tossed it to the table because it was so hot. "Oh, okay. I understand, but that's not that many, right? I mean, how many people would each house have? One or two?"

"Well, they are rich." Hugh thought back to some of the larger, more expensive homes he had broken into. "They may have two or three people. A cook, a maid, a butler." He shrugged. "Probably not a gardener. And if they have a driver, they will be wherever the rich person works."

Isaac moved to the table and picked up his used fork. "Exactly. And they are probably just interested in doing their job so the only ones that would even be interested in you will be the one in that woman's house. Cy?" Issac blew on the chili.

"Yes. Cy." Hugh said. "Well, how's the chili?"

Isaac made a face. "It doesn't taste like much either." He reached for the container of spice. "I don't think I care for this food at all."

"It probably gets the job done." Hugh said.

"What?"

"It just fills your belly." Hugh explained. "And gives you nourishment. That's it."

"Proximity alert." Cynthia said. "There are two vessels approaching that will be within one hundred thousand miles in one minute."

"Are they flying together?" Hugh asked.

"I do not understand the question."

Hugh exhaled. "Are the two ships flying on the same vector towards us or are there just two ships coming from different directions towards us? Are the ships associated with each other or are they just two individual ships?" Between the two, Hugh hoped it was two unaffiliated ships approaching instead of two ships working together. His flight training on the *Giselle* did not include any weapons training because the ship did not have any at all. And the only shielding it had was electro-static shielding for navigational purposes; micro asteroids and dust; not for the ballistic weapons or missiles that other ships were probably equipped with.

"They are both flying on the same vector." Cynthia clarified.

"Where are they flying from?" Hugh stood. "Finish your meal then put this stuff away. I'm going to go see who these people are."

"Their flight path suggests they originated from Mars." Cynthia said. "However, they could have made course corrections so they could have originated from anywhere."

"Great." Hugh said as he moved quickly to the cockpit.

"One of the ships is hailing us." Cynthia said.

"Oh, this gets better and better." Hugh scowled as he stepped into the cockpit.

Three

Abigail walked into the clearing where the ship had been earlier that evening. The area was quiet- it always struck her as odd that it seemed to take several days for animals to return to the area after one of the Gatherer's ships left.

As she walked across where the ship had sat, she looked up at the blue sky, wondering how Hugh was doing. Suddenly she stumbled as her feet pulled out from under her. Caught off guard, she let go of her walking stick and put her hands out to catch herself. Instead of crashing to the ground, she fell slowly, touching with her hands gently. Alarmed, Abigail crab walked several steps backward then stood. She watched as her stick fell in slow motion onto the ground as well.

"Gravity." She said out loud. Hugh had explained how it worked but she still didn't really understand it. Slowly and while watching the ground, she moved forward to where the ship had sat. As she got closer, she felt lighter. Much, much lighter. She carefully bent over and picked up her thick walking stick. When she reached the middle of the area where the ship had been, she jumped upward, rising almost five feet in the air. She flailed her arms out as she panicked, fully expecting to fall in a heap to the ground. Instead, she floated down gently.

"Oh!" She said when her feet touched the ground. "That is most alarming." Abigail moved carefully out of the area where the ship had sat, until her steps felt normal again. She circled around toward a large grey piece of fabric that had been tossed to the side. It seemed to have been left behind by both the Humans and Hugh. She wondered if it would have some use back in town. When she got to it, she picked up a corner of it to feel it- it was lightweight but seemed sturdy. She held it up to the light but couldn't see through it, making her believe it was waterproof. "This could be handy to make some jackets for when it rains." She remarked as she pulled the tarp up even more to examine it more closely. There was quite a bit of it- enough for a dozen jackets even.

As she pulled the tarp up, the body of Baxter came into view. He had been stabbed in the chest.

"Oh, Hugh." Abigail said. "Oh, Hugh why?" She pulled back the tarp further to reveal Carl; he had also been stabbed. She hadn't actually asked what had happened to the four people that were on the ship, but had assumed at the time that they were being held inside while Hugh was learning how to fly the ship. Now that she thought back, she realized it was odd that she never saw them after that first night over the two days the ship was there in the clearing. "Oh Hugh." She let out a long breath.

A movement on the far side of the tarp made her jump. Fearing that some sort of animal had gotten under it, she quietly lowered the corner she was holding and side-stepped around the tarp. Abigail tightened her grip on her walking stick as she moved to the far side where the tarp was moving slightly. She bent down and eased the stick under it. It was longer than her at six feet and was an inch thick. After half of it was under the tarp, she flipped it back, expecting to see a surprised racoon.

She gasped as she stumbled back, end of the stick dragging in the dirt as she tried to keep her balance.

A very obviously dead woman swiveled her eyes over and looked at Abigail then narrowed her eyes. She wasn't able to move her head or speak because her head seemed to be only held in place by several tendrils of sinew. She opened her mouth revealing two large teeth very similar to Hugh's. Blood had run down the side of her cheek and had dried there. She grimaced at Abigail.

"Oh! Oh no! Another one!" Abigal said as she brought her stick up to defend herself.

The woman went back to chewing on the dead Baxter's arm. There was a bit of it missing.

"What on Earth?" Abigail said as she moved closer to the woman. As she watched, another sinew ran from her body up to her head and attached itself. Where it had started from was new, pink skin. Realization hit her; Hugh had obviously cut off her head to prevent her from becoming a vampire, like he had said needed to be done to Benfleet. But when he moved them all under the tarp, her head must have been close enough to the body to touch it, which was close enough to start reattaching thanks to the vampirism. 'I am very hard to kill' Hugh had said. And now that it could feed on the dead man, it was healing itself. "No, no, no." Abigail said as she looked around, unsure what to do. She remembered that Hugh had burned Benfleet, but didn't understand why he had not done the same with this woman. She looked down at the woman again. *Blood. Hugh had to drink blood. Perhaps since this is a dead person she is eating, it doesn't help her recover as quickly. That's why she has been like this for those two days instead of completely healed.* A shudder ran through her as she thought about this woman vampire rampaging in the area like Benfleet had.

Abigail looked toward town- two miles away. When she looked back at the woman, another strand of sinew had started moving toward her head like a whisp of fabric moving in the breeze. There were only a dozen of them attached so far but she could see where the woman's esophagus and trachea were also growing towards the head. Abigail was worried that in the time it would take her to get to town and back, the woman might be strong enough to stand on her own. Stand and fight. Or worse- feed quicker. Abigail considered her dash to town. Not only would she have to get there, she would have to find someone who understood what a vampire was and bring them back as well- it would take a great deal of time.

"Hugh, we are going to have words when you get back." Abigail said. "*Words*." She approached the feeding vampire tentatively; the last thing she wanted to do was get so close the vampire could grab her. She kept her walking stick out and at the ready.

Abigail had used the stick defensively twice before; once dealing with a wolf that tried to attack her, and later against an overly inquisitive racoon. She had considered sharpening the end after the incident with the wolf but then decided against it. Carrying a walking stick was fine; carrying a weapon around town was definitely something the elders would frown upon.

As Abigail stepped closer to the vampire, it stopped feeding and stared at her.

Abigail pointed at the woman. "You will not succeed." She said. "You are dead and need to remain that way." Abigail held her walking stick out, reaching for Cy's head. "You are not natural!"

Cy tried to grab the end of the stick. Since she was unable to turn her head to see her own hand, she couldn't judge the distance properly and swung wide with her hand.

The sinew connected.

Abigail sidestepped to put herself out of the vampire's line of sight then looked around the area. There was quite a bit of dead fall wood around the area; probably put there by the gatherers to use during their stay. None of it was very big so she could handle the pieces easily. She looked at the two men. They seemed to be completely dead thanks to having just been stabbed. Abigail looked at the third man; the one that the woman was chewing on. *If she became a vampire because Hugh bit her, then this other man might become one too since this woman has bitten him.* She stepped forward to examine the man more closely, trying to see if he was moving on his own. "Oh!" Abigail called out as she hopped over the reaching hand that brushed her foot. "Stop that!" She skidded to a stop out of reach even though the hand continued to blindly flail about trying to grab her. Abigal walked over to the head. Its eyes swiveled around to look at her and it grimaced again. "Vile creature." She held her stick out. "You are a vile creature but I pity you. Therefore, I will put you out of your misery and let God deal with you." She let out a long breath then scanned the area looking at the deadwood. "A roaring fire will do it, I'm sure." She looked from the woman to the forest twice. "I'll be right back." Abigail said as she stuck her walking stick into the ground then scooted around the area selecting larger dead branches that would burn the hottest. It took her several minutes to get an armful before returning to the tarp. A movement made her look back at the tarp. The third man's leg twitched. "No, no no!" She said as she rushed forward and dumped the load of wood on top of him. "Not two of you!" She ran back out to the perimeter of the clearing grabbing wood and dumping it onto the third man. She looked at the wood piled on the tarp. *Waste not.* With a relegated sigh, she grabbed the tarp and pulled it out from between the corpses and the wood, dragging it a safe distance away. She returned to gathering wood and piling it. When she had a large pile, she bent down and used her knife to scrape at one of the larger branches, making a pile of wood pulp. Using the back of her knife on her striker, she started the small pile of pulp on fire. Abigail carefully blew on the glowing embers as she added larger sticks. Once she had a small flame, she used it on the larger sticks. Within minutes, she had a good-sized fire going on top of the third man. "That will do, I think." She gave a curt nod as she turned to look for larger pieces of wood to keep the fire burning longer. "Yes, that will do nicely."

As she gathered wood, she had a terrible thought- she spun around, and looked at the other two bodies. *She could eat them as well!* Abigail stepped closer to them to see if they were moving but was afraid to get too close, even though they appeared to only have been stabbed. "Oh bother." She said with a frown. "Brother Hugh, you are in for it when you get home." She let out a long breath then grabbed one of the men by his feet and dragged him towards the fire.

The fire was too hot for her to get very close to it so she pulled the man alongside it, then rolled him into the edge of it. When she got him there, she did the same thing with the other man, positioning him on the other side of the fire. *Now to get more wood to make sure they all burn up.*

Abigail did another circuit of the clearing picking up long branches which she dumped on the men, bringing the fire on top of them. She wiped her brow with her shirtsleeve then turned to get more wood to keep in reserve in case the fire burned down before the bodies were completely incinerated. Large branches however were getting harder to find. She looked across the clearing to see if there were any in that direction. She was shocked to notice that the woman was now missing. "Oh no!" She quickly looked around the clearing.

The woman was standing with her hand on Abigail's walking stick for support. While her head wasn't properly on the top of her neck, it had enough sinew attached that while it was still at an odd angle, it was facing forward. It still couldn't speak but instead bared her teeth at Abigail.

"Oh no!" Abigail backed up. The flames were hot so she sidestepped away from it, keeping an eye on the woman. "Keep away from me!" Abigail commanded.

The woman started toward Abigail, using the stick for support as it went.

Four

"What kind of ships are they?" Hugh asked. "Military ships? Law enforcement?"

"They are commuter ships."

"Like this one?"

"One is larger, one is smaller. But they are privately owned ships like this one." Cynthia said. "The *Aram Chaos* and the *Iani Chaos Two*."

"Similar names. Are they from the same place?" Hugh asked.

"They are from adjacent mining colonies on Mars located along the equator. The name Aram Chaos comes from an ancient term for Syria and was originally assigned…"

"Stop, stop, stop." Hugh said. "Stop explaining Cynthia. Are the two ships still heading toward us?"

"They are on an intercept course."

A thought occurred to Hugh. "Could they also be on course for Earth?"

"The two ships are on the proper trajectory for travel between Mars and Earth due to their current positions." Cynthia said.

"Great. Who is hailing us? Is it the big ship or the small ship? How big are these ships?"

"The *Iani Chaos Two* is hailing us. It is the larger of the two ships at four thousand two hundred tons. The *Aram Chaos* weighs two thousand one hundred tons."

"What do we weigh?" Hugh asked, trying to get an idea on the size of the ships.

"The *Giselle* weighs two thousand two hundred tons." Cynthia replied.

"Okay, open communication with the *Iani Chaos Two*," Hugh said.

Isaac entered the cockpit. "I got everything put away. There is a bin back there that…"

Hugh turned and held a finger up to his lips. "Shhh." He said softly.

"Unidentified ship, this is the *Iani Chaos Two*, do you read?" A voice said over the speaker.

"*Iani Chaos we read*," Hugh said, picking up a calm pilot-tone to his voice. It was something most every pilot did when talking on the radio; it was a cool and relaxed tone- even if the airplane had lost all engine power and was on fire. "This is the *Giselle*, sorry about that. Comms were offline. We read you." He gestured for Isaac to sit in the copilot seat as he pressed the mute button on the microphone. "Don't say anything Isaac. I have no idea if these people know the people who used to own this ship." He increased the ship's speed by twenty percent then took his finger off the mute button. "Go ahead."

"Just checking who was flying out here in the dark, *Giselle*." The man responded.

"Oh. Turned off our transponder while we were down." Hugh said. "I thought the copilot got it back on. And he thought I did."

"It happens." The voice said. "Good haul?"

Hugh's eyes got large; he wasn't sure what the man was talking about. He looked at Isaac.

"Yes. We got her." Isaac said. "We are heading back to Deimos now." He looked at Hugh and smiled wide. "So how are things with you?"

Hugh waved a hand at Isaac to quiet him, even though he was glad the young man had the presence of mind to understand the question.

"We are picking up a couple of Aboriginals. Got a special request." The man said. After a moment he added, "Where's Carl and Baxter?"

Hugh cringed. When Isaac opened his mouth to answer, Hugh slapped him on the shoulder. "Carl is in the galley." He said quickly. "He's buying another ship so he took us on a run with him to learn the ropes."

"Old Carl's expanding, huh?" The man replied

"Yup." Hugh said. "It'll be Commodore Carl next time you see him."

"Good for him. Have a safe flight and tell him that Schiaparelli says to stop serving slop to his passengers, *Giselle*."

Hugh laughed. "Oh, we've already eaten so I agree with you there. Might as well serve dirt."

"Roger that. Oh, and whatever you do, pass on the chili."

"Will do. Good hunting *Iani Chaos Two*." Hugh reached out toward the 'close communication' icon.

"Giovanni. Giovanni Schiaparelli." The man said.

"Bob. Bob Pardo." Hugh said, using the name of a famous Vietnam pilot that all his flight instructors invariably talked about. "First drinks are on me when we get to Mars."

"That's a deal, Bob." Giovanni said.

"A done deal. *Giselle* out." Hugh tapped the button and it greyed out. "Oh man, I'm glad that pilots are still pilots." He looked at Isaac. "Nicely done, Brother Isaac. He caught me completely off guard. What made you think of Abigail?"

"Well, if they were heading toward Earth then they are probably doing the same thing; gathering people. And I figured if they were doing that, then they probably knew other gatherers. Just like carpenters all seem to know each other."

Hugh leaned back in his seat. "Very nicely done."

Isaac put his hand to his belly. "He was right about skipping the chili. It has my stomach upset."

"Well maybe when we get to Cy's place, we can grab some food when we get Gideon."

"That is a good idea." Isaac's stomach made a gurgling sound. "Oh, excuse me." He said as he stood quickly.

"I have this up here. You go lay down for a little bit. This processed food probably won't sit well with you no matter the quality." Hugh said- everything the Amish ate was either fresh, or freshly canned with no preservatives at all. He had to admit that the spaghetti was also not sitting well with him. He had eaten just to keep up appearances but would skip meals from now on. Especially on the *Giselle*. The medical supplies were still an option, however.

Five

The vampire lurched forward, her legs apparently not working as well as they should. The stick kept her from falling over as she approached Abigail.

Abigail looked left and right- she had used most all the longer branches on the fire- which was now roaring hot. There were some longer ones but they were behind the vampire. Gathering up her skirt, she ran in an arc around to where the longer branches were. She looked back- the vampire had turned and was starting in her direction, eyes hungrily trained on her.

"Oh dear!" Abigail looked down at the branches. Compared to her straight and polished birch walking stick, they all looked woefully inadequate. She picked up stick after stick, only to break it when she tested it. She looked back- the vampire was a mere twenty feet away and still advancing. Abigail broke another stick then threw the two halves at the vampire.

The vampire didn't even flinch as one of the sticks bounced off her side.

"Oh dear!" Abigail ran to the side to another pile of sticks. The first one she grabbed was two inches thick and almost five feet long. It had several branches sticking out of it so she stood it upright and hopped on the lower ones, breaking them off.

The vampire turned and started toward her again.

"No, no no!" She said as she moved quicker at breaking off the small outcropping branches. "No you don't!" When she got half way up the stick, she turned it over and began to step on the two branches forming a 'v' at the top, then stopped herself. She looked at the vampire- she was within ten feet and had one arm outstretched. The other was still holding the walking stick for support.

Abigail turned the branch over putting the forked end out. The fire was over to the left of the two of them so she sidestepped to the right as she jabbed the stick at the vampire, keeping her at bay.

When Abigail was lined up with the vampire between her and the fire, she rushed forward, catching her in the 'v'. She pushed, causing the vampire to stumble backward. Not wanting her to fall over and perhaps roll away, she pushed slowly and steadily as the vampire took shuffling steps backwards. She did not seem to be aware of the fire at all.

The vampire made another soundless grimace at Abigail and dropped the stick. She reached out with both hands and grabbed the stick trying to wrestle it away.

"All right then, you vile creature." Abigail said. "It is time you stopped this!" She gave a final push, toppling the vampire over into the raging fire.

The vampire never looked back as she fell. With her head hanging from a strands of flesh she kept her eyes trained on Abigail the entire time until she was flat on her back in the raging fire. The small branches gave way and she sank into it. Only then did she start to thrash to try to get out but Abigail kept pushing her down with the stick until the vampire finally lay still as the fire consumed her.

Abigail jogged quickly to the side and grabbed a bunch of sticks then threw them on top of the vampire- who was completely engulfed in flames.

"Oh." Was all Abigail managed to say as she retrieved her trusty stick, stumbled back several feet away from the heat of the fire then sat down hard. She watched the flames for movement but there was none.

After a few minutes, Eli came into view.

"Brother Eli!" Abigail called. "Oh, where were you a half hour ago!"

"I was tending the animals since we have lost Isaac for the moment." Eli said with a smile. "What is wrong, Sister Abigail?" He looked around. "And why do you have a raging fire going out here in the middle of the day?"

"Oh, Brother Eli." Abigail shook her head. "I can't imagine you will believe me, but I'll tell you anyway." She said. "I'll have to tell you while we wait here because we have to make sure the fire burns down completely."

Eli nodded. "Forest fires." He said knowingly. "They are very dangerous."

"Forest fires?" Abigail laughed. "Vampires, Brother Eli. *Vampires!*"

Six

Hugh stepped out of the berth he had been sleeping in. He had the lights in the ship turned down low and set to a navy-blue color. For some reason the white lights bothered him after a while so after a discussion with Isaac, it was decided that blue tinted lights were the best choice for the both of them.

Isaac was sitting at the table drinking a coffee. It was something he had never had before. While the Amish people Hugh had lived with before cherished their coffee, the ones he knew now lived much too far north to ever cultivate it. Tea was their preferred choice of hot drink. Chocolate was also something the Anchorage Amish people had never had since that was also a tropical plant. "I told you that wasn't a good idea." Hugh said with a smile.

"It's really good." Isaac replied.

"Yes, coffee is a great drink but you can't grow it where you live so you shouldn't get used to it." Hugh said.

"I know." Isaac replied. "But it's so delicious."

Hugh considered that for a moment. "Cynthia. Do they drink coffee on Mars or Venus? Or the other planets?"

"Coffee is a morning staple within the Solar System." Cynthia said. "It is also drunk with dessert and often throughout the day."

"Great." Isaac said. He looked at his cup.

"How much coffee can you get from one coffee plant?" Hugh asked.

No one answered.

Hugh frowned. "*Cynthia*, how much coffee can you get from one coffee plant?"

"A typical coffee tree yield in a season is ten pounds of coffee cherry which equates to one pound of roasted coffee." Cynthia replied.

"Wow, that's a whole lot of trees you'd have to have, to keep a thousand people in coffee." Hugh said as he looked at Isaac. "That's just way too much coffee for you to try and grow. Oh. Cynthia, at what temperature does a coffee tree die? Low temperature that is."

"A coffee tree will die if the temperature drops below twelve degrees Celsius."

"Celsius? What is that in Fahrenheit?"

"Fahrenheit. Okay. That is fifty-five degrees Fahrenheit." Cynthia replied.

"That settles it." Hugh said. "I'm sorry Isaac, there is no way for your town to grow coffee; it gets way too cold and you can't just build greenhouses because it would take a thousand trees to make enough coffee for everyone. It just wouldn't work. And I'm not sure I'd just be able to run into the corner store on Mars and buy a thousand pounds of coffee every month."

"Maybe I could just drink it on the *Giselle*?" Isaac asked.

"No, Isaac. We have discussed this." Hugh sat at the table. "Modern technology and Amish do not mix. It never has. This is a one-time instance right now." He put his hands flat on the table. "You are here… *We* are here to get Abigail's husband back for her. After that, you are going back to your work in the town."

"How will you fly the ship alone?" Isaac asked.

"I'll figure something out." Hugh said. "Or I won't take the ship anywhere that requires me to have to sleep. Either way, I won't be taking you on any more adventures into space."

"Okay." Isaac said, crestfallen.

"Do you understand why?"

Isaac nodded. "I suppose so. Brother Eli also explained it to me."

"It's part of the life of an Amish person, Isaac. I've lived with Amish people before and except for rare instances, they did not use modern technology. It is a distraction."

"Rare instances?" Isaac smiled.

"Yes, like this one-time rare instance." Hugh said. The Amish he had known had used freezers at neighbor's homes in return for some of the meat. They would also use a phone at a neighbor's house if there was an emergency. "And there won't be any more discussion about it. Once we are back home, you are going back to your life as it was before I showed up." He reached across the table and took Isaac's coffee cup. "So, no more coffee."

"Fine." Isaac said.

"Proximity Alert." Cynthia said. "Destination approaching."

"Here we go again." Isaac lamented. "Who is it this time?"

"No, no. This alert is for us being close to Deimos." Hugh said. "I set it up last night."

"Oh. So, we're finally there?"

"We could have been there in two hours from Earth." Hugh smiled. "But thanks to my intelligent partner, we took a longer path there, so we are now arriving at nine thirty in the morning; when most people should be at work."

"Right." Isaac said with a smile. "That is true. Because when I take care of the animals…" He began.

"Yes, I know." Hugh cut him off. "Now let's get up front so I can go through what you need to do once we land and you're alone in the ship."

Isaac glanced at the coffee cup.

"For starters, you won't be drinking coffee." Hugh said. He gulped down what was left in the cup. It was sickly sweet. "What have you done to this coffee? It tastes like syrup." He put the cup down, stood and pointed at it. "That, brother is a sin."

Isaac's eyes got large. "What?" He stood as well. "I mean, I didn't know that I wasn't supposed…"

Hugh put his hand on Isaac's shoulder. "I'm joking. It isn't an actual sin. It's more a tragedy, now that I think about it."

"Oh. Good." Isaac said, relieved.

"Let's go. We need to find a place to land." Hugh said.

Seven

The ship passed slowly over the rocky surface of Deimos. Mars loomed massively in the sky above it- the moon was a mere twelve thousand miles away from its parent planet. The other moon, Phobos was even closer; five thousand miles away. In contrast, Earth's moon was a much more respectable two hundred thirty-eight thousand miles away.

"I don't understand." Isaac said as he moved the viewscreen around looking at the surface.

"What's that?" Hugh was looking at telemetry readouts and not paying attention to the images of the surface.

"You said that there were a hundred people living on Deimos, and I understand that's not a lot for such a big place, but I don't see anything that looks like houses."

"They live underground." Hugh said. "They have hollowed out parts of Deimos to make a bunch of rooms. Then they filled them with oxygen so they can breathe inside."

"Like the caves back home?"

Hugh smirked. "Yes, like caves. Sorry about that. Then using the same method they use to make the ship move, they have made the gravity higher here so that it is the same as on Mars. That way they can move around and live in an environment they are familiar with."

Isaac chuckled. "Even after you explain it, I don't understand how they do it."

"I don't really understand how their ships move either if that helps." Hugh said as he glanced at the viewscreens in front of his seat. "There. See that? That's the house we want."

"Where? Where are you pointing?" Isaac pushed his finger around the screen panning that camera around.

"Straight ahead but to the left. That tall looking thing. It even has square corners and a flat roof with a long point sticking out of it. That's the top of the house we are going to. We've passed three others so far. See it? It's sticking up out of the ground."

"Oh, yes. I see that now." Isaac smiled. "That wasn't what I was expecting at all." The structure ahead was a single tall spire sticking up out of the surface of the moon, almost like a tall thin pyramid with a large square base. "And one family lives in that? That is really big."

"Well, most of the living area is actually underground. That part is a landing place for this ship and whatever other ships they own so it's a big empty storage area. Communication antenna, that sort of thing." Hugh explained.

"And you're going to land inside that?"

"No. No way. I'd end up running into the side of it. Maybe after flying this thing for a few months, I'd try landing inside. Now? No way. I'm going to land across the valley from it, a mile or so away then walk in."

"How are you going to get there? In one of those silver space suits you showed me?"

Hugh nodded. "Yes. There's one that sort of fits me. It will be wrinkly on the legs and arms but it will work."

"What about Gideon? How will he get back? You said there is no air out there. Why don't you go from the underground where there is air?"

"Because I'd have to maneuver this ship through a tiny opening and I'd probably fail at it. Then we'd either get caught, or destroy this ship." Hugh explained. "Landing on a nice open flat space is the best chance we have at having a ship that will fly us back home when we're ready to leave."

"But he doesn't have a silver space suit."

"There will be plenty of them inside the house, I'm sure." Hugh said. "Even if it's big on him it will still keep him alive. Plus, with the ship way out here, the chances of anyone coming over to talk to you are small. It probably won't even get noticed."

"That makes sense." Isaac frowned. "But... if someone does come over?"

"You tell them what I said; that you don't know how to operate the ship, you're just a passenger and they will have to come back later. Then don't answer them no matter what they say."

"That seems a little rude." Isaac said.

"These people put other people in cages for their *entertainment*, I'm not worried about being a little rude to them." Hugh pointed. "There. That's a nice flat spot right there." He pressed several icons. "Lowering gear and setting down." He shook his head. "Here goes nothing."

Eight

Hugh stepped out of the *Giselle* onto the surface of Deimos. His space suit bunched up on his legs and arms instead of being smooth but even so, everything sealed tightly. He looked up at Mars- it was massive in the sky. And very close. He could see several dozen blue areas on it that were ostensibly geo-domes. If they were visible from this distance, Hugh realized they would have to be hundreds of miles across. The sight was awesome. "How far you've come, Hugh." He said.

"What's that?" Isaac asked.

"Oh, I was just standing here looking up at Mars in this space suit from the surface of this little moon and thinking how I started out in Jamestown Colony not knowing much about anything." He smirked. "And realizing just now I still don't know much about anything. Not a damn thing, really."

"Oh, uhm…" Isaac said worriedly. "Are you sure you are okay?"

"Yes, sorry. It is just a lot to take in." He looked across the small valley at the structure on the horizon. Since Deimos was only seven and a half miles in diameter, the distance was deceiving; it looked like it should have been a dozen miles away but it was really just over a mile. "Heading that way now." Hugh started to walk but had a hard time at it. Even though the gravity of the tiny moon had been increased to that of Mars, it was still less than forty percent of the gravity of Earth so instead of weighing a hundred seventy-five pounds, Hugh weighed sixty-six pounds. He tried skipping as he had seen a character do in a movie he had seen- another Human who found himself on Mars- and found that it actually worked pretty well. "Hugh Carter, a fighting man of Mars." Hugh said as he continued to skip toward the building in fifty-foot leaps.

"I didn't think you had a last name." Isaac said. "That you remembered, anyway."

"I don't. This just reminded me of something from a long time ago. It was a story about this man that ends up on Mars and he has to deal with the gravity being different than what he is used to. It was written by a man named Edgar Rice Burroughs." Hugh slipped as he hit the ground and tumbled to a stop. He looked up at the dark sky then toward the sun- it was a small reddish colored circle near the edge of Mars. Soon it would be behind it and even the dim twilight would be gone completely. He was relieved that even with the sun in view, it did not seem to affect him as it did from Earth. It was far enough away he didn't even need to have the sun shield down on his helmet. "Are you able to track me?"

After a moment, Isaac answered: "Yes, I can see you on the map you set up. And I see the house. You are... a mile from it right now."

"Okay. Keep an eye on me because when it gets dark, I might wander off course so you'll have to tell me left or right to get me there."

"Right. I remember." Isaac said. "You're doing great right now, heading straight for it."

"Do you see anything else on the screen besides me?"

"No."

Hugh started to ask Isaac to ask Cynthia if there were any other ships in the area but then he decided that even if there were, there was nothing they could do about it. Before leaving the ship, he had turned off the transponder again and shut down as many systems as Cynthia said he safely could to reduce their electronic signature to almost nothing. He had also made sure Isaac knew how to turn on the safety overrides so no one could open a hatch from the outside. None of it made him feel any better when the ship's hatch closed behind him and he was alone on Deimos. "Well, keep an eye out. I'm going to try to get to the house before I lose all my sunlight."

"Right." Isaac said again.

Hugh sped up his skipping, gobbling up the distance between him and the structure within minutes thanks to hundred-foot leaps. He wasn't worried if anyone saw him; it was probably how everyone got around on the tiny moon when they weren't in a surface vehicle.

By the time he made it to the bottom of the building, it was completely dark around him.

"Hugh?" Isaac said softly.

"What is it, Isaac?"

"You're there." Isaac whispered.

"You don't have to whisper; no one can hear you but me." Hugh smiled. "But thanks. It looks like there is a door over on the side of this thing. I'm going to go inside. I don't know if I'll still be able to talk to you once I'm inside the building so don't panic if you don't hear from me for a while."

"Oh. I…" Isaac began. "What is a while?"

"It's not that big of a place." Hugh looked up at the tall spire. "I don't know; an hour?" He considered that. "Tell you what, let's make it two. If you don't hear back from me in two hours, just go back to Earth."

"I don't know how to fly this thing." Isaac sounded panicked. "I… you have to come back!"

"I've saved the flight instructions for you. It won't be a picture-perfect flight, but all you have to do is ask Cynthia to give you the flight instructions for Earth and she will say them in order for you to follow. Push the buttons she tells you to push."

"How will I remember them all?" Panic rose in Isaac's voice. "But you can't just leave me…"

"Isaac. Listen." Hugh said. "*Just listen.* My plan is for me to get back to the ship and fly back to Earth with you and Gideon. That's my plan, but sometimes plans go wrong. But in case that happens." He emphasized it. "*In case that happens*, you can follow the instructions I gave to Cynthia. She will tell them to you one at a time. Once you do one step, she will give you the next one. She can tell you how to do it, she just can't press the buttons herself. Understand?"

"Okay, but … you're coming back, right?"

"I really plan on it, Isaac." Hugh said. He pressed the button on the exterior hatch. As Cynthia had said, since the suit belonged to someone from the house, the door unlocked and opened, bathing him in red light. "Okay, I'm going inside."

"Okay. So in an hour…" Isaac began.

"Whoa, whoa, whoa. It's two hours. *Two hours.*" Hugh said. "Repeat that back to me. Two hours."

"Two hours. So noon." Isaac said.

"Right." He considered that. "Unless you hear from me, right? Don't just plan on taking off at noon without trying to reach me."

"Oh, right, right. Of course I'll try to talk to you first." Isaac said even though his voice didn't sound like he had considered that.

"Oh man." Hugh shook his head. "Okay. I'm going in. It's ten ten. So twelve ten."

"Right."

With a relegated sign, Hugh stepped into the airlock and pressed the inner button. The outer door sealed. After the airlock filled with air, the lights changed to green. "Green is go." Hugh said. "At least that's still the same." He tilted his head upward. "Hey Isaac; can you hear me?"

"I… hear…. Some." He got in reply.

Hugh looked at the button to open the inner door then decided to take off the space suit first. His original plan was to just wear the suit into the home, grab Gideon then make a run for it. Then he thought that if he were in a space suit walking around, it might garner unwanted attention. When he tried on the suit and discovered it was far too big, he left his clothes on so it would be less bulky- even his shoes.

Since he had clothes on, he removed the flight suit with the diagonal zipper across the front and rolled it up. He opened the bins that were placed in the side of the small area. The first three had suits in them. The fourth was empty so he put his there. He checked the fifth one- there was a suit in there as well. "There we go, Gideon; you'll even get your choice of suits." He pushed the bin shut. Before hanging his helmet on the peg with the others, he removed the two-way radio headset from it. "Isaac, can you hear me?"

"…Hear…. Not really… It's." Isaac replied.

Hugh frowned and opened the inner door. He peeked around it as it swung open. The corridor was empty. When he pushed the door shut again, he slipped the headset on and pressed the 'talk' button. "Isaac, can you hear me at all?"

This time he got no response. "Two hours to go." He said as he looked left and right. From what Cynthia had told him the buildings were multi-level apartment complexes with three or four families in each one. Only two super-rich families had their own private building; two politicians. Neither was the governor of Mars or even Deimos; the moon did not have enough people on it to warrant a Mayor or other leader. According to Cynthia, police forces were present on Mars but Phobos the larger moon only had two private security officers; Deimos had one. She had also provided Hugh with a map of the complex. He reached into his pocket and pulled it out. Unfolding it, he turned it around to get his bearings. He looked behind him- the airlock had 'AL 6-01' on it in large stenciled letters. He turned the map again so the number six airlock was behind him. That meant that the Rollins portion of the building was to the left.

Hugh looked right. There were two family areas in that direction. He didn't know if they also kept 'living art' and with a two-hour window, he could not risk searching both of those residences before going to where he knew Gideon was. "Next time. I'll get you next time." Hugh said as he started to the left.

Nine

Abigail stepped into the clearing. There was a large black mark, a pile of ashes, and several white bones where the fire had been the day before.

"They're all gone." Eli said as he moved beside her.

"I know. I just…" She looked at him. "Thank you."

"It was a harrowing experience, I'm sure." Eli said. "Accompanying you here is no problem at all, Sister Abigail."

"I just wanted to get that cloth. I think it will make good rain jackets." She gestured at the pile of tan cloth. It was still piled up where she had dragged it. "Will you help me fold it?"

Eli nodded. "Surely I will." He grasped a corner and pulled it closer to the middle of the clearing. As he went, Abigail stopped to watch him.

"What?" Eli said self-consciously. "What is it?"

"Oh." She smiled. "When I came here the morning after they left, the ground under where their craft was... was... strange. I was lighter there."

"You were covered with light?"

"No. I felt lighter. I could jump very high and tripped when I walked as if my weight was being held up by strings."

Eli sighed. "These are very strange things that have come into our life." He said warily.

"And not always good things, yes I know." Abigail picked up an opposite corner. She looked at the other end. "This is not made like a sheet at all." She held her end up. "It has sides on it, like it was made to contain something. Water perhaps?"

"Perhaps. A portable pool of water. This is much larger than a tub." Eli shook his head. "I don't know why anyone would want something this big to soak in. Strange indeed."

"In any case, it will make good clothes for when it rains, I think." Abigail walked over and picked up another corner. "If we fold in the sides, we can make it a square again to fold it better."

"That is a good idea." Eli said. "And while we fold this up, we can talk."

Abigail nodded toward the pile of ashes. "About that?"

"You were fortunate to not have been hurt, or killed even." Eli said as he lay the fabric down with the side folded in. He moved to the other corner to do the same. "It was very careless of Hugh to allow this to happen."

"Oh no." Abigail said quickly. "I don't think he did it on purpose, Brother Eli."

Eli smirked. "I understand how he reminds you of Elam." He said, referring to her dead brother. "But he isn't, you know."

"Oh, I know that." Abigail said. "I understand that. I'm just glad I was in a position to help him is all."

"Help him?"

"I think I've made him a better person."

Eli gestured at the scorched area. "There were four bodies here that would say otherwise, I think." He nodded at the far corner as he picked up his corner. "That side first. We take it a third of the way."

Abigail went to that corner and picked it up. Together they carried that edge toward the middle, folding the large tarp over.

"Sister Abigail, Hugh is not like us. Not at all." He hesitated. "I am not sure if I should even mention it but…" He shook his head. "Never mind." He gestured. "The other two corners now to where it meets this fold."

Abigail followed to the other corner. "What? What shouldn't you mention? Is it gossip?"

"It is not gossip." Eli said. "Because I have verified that it has actually happened, these events."

"What is that then?" Abigail said as she moved the cloth over to meet where the other side had been put.

"Well," Eli said. "There was this hunting party. For Mastodons. And they didn't come back."

"It is a dangerous hunt. They are large and wild. And intelligent." Abigail said. She had known of several people who were killed and others that were hurt hunting the beasts.

"But of these seven experienced men, none returned alive. None. And it was just before Hugh walked to our fire. It is more than a coincidence."

"No, Hugh could not have killed those men." Abigail said. She tugged on the two folded edges, stretching out the cloth.

"Once over to make it flat." Eli said. "Why? It was before we had even met him. Before we befriended him, and he us."

"No, that isn't possible. Not Hugh." Abigail said as she folded the tarp over, completing the one-third fold.

"It is more than possible, Sister; it is likely. Now I do not want to confront him on this issue. And I don't think you should either."

"Then what are you suggesting?"

"I think that once Hugh returns. We have a celebration and then bid him farewell. If he returns that is." Eli said. "I will roll to you. Keep it tight." He said as he began rolling the tarp.

Abigail bent down and began tugging on the two edges of the tarp. "What if he doesn't want to leave?"

Eli looked up at her as he rolled. "We will thank him for his assistance and knowledge. Then tell him goodbye. I think he will understand. He isn't blind to what we are and what he is."

"But we are supposed to love the sinner, not the sin."

"The sin is *murder*, Sister." Eli said. "And not just one. If we go with what we have right in front of us, we have eleven murders. *Eleven*. I just cannot condone that kind of behavior. How can I?"

"Eleven." Abigail repeated softly. There had never been a murder between the Amish in the town for as long as anyone could remember. The people in town did die of old age, sickness, and of course hunting accidents. The wilderness was a dangerous place. Not to mention the hostile people who lived around them. So people were killed. But no one in town killed anyone else. Ever. "I understand what you are saying." Abigail stood as Eli reached her. "But he told me he was only hunting animals now. He gave me his word he won't kill anyone else."

"Else?" Eli stood. "Where; here? What about where he is right now; on Mars?" He pointed at the sky. "What about up there?" He put his hands on his hips. "Tell me Sister Abigail, will you revel at the return of your husband?"

"Of course I will! It has been two years."

"What if his freedom came at the cost of other's lives? What if getting Gideon back means that Hugh will kill a dozen people up there?"

"A dozen? Now that is unlikely, Brother Eli. Because…"

"Okay then, Sister." Eli cut her off. "How many murders *is* acceptable for the return of your husband?"

Abigail looked up at the dark, cloudy sky. "Oh. I…" her voice trailed off as tears filled her eyes. "Oh, no that won't happen." She looked at Eli and shook her head.. "No. No he would not."

"How are you so sure?"

"I spoke with Hugh about this. Specifically. I asked him to make sure no one got hurt when he tried to rescue Gideon. Even if it meant leaving him behind." She looked up at the sky. "So he…" Her voice trailed off.

Eli was now upset with himself for even broaching the subject. He had planned to just talk to Hugh one-on-one about the situation when he returned, then have him quietly leave on the space craft. "Sister Abigail, I am sorry for even bringing it up." Eli said. "Really, if it did happen it would not be your fault in any case. Because you didn't ask him to go get your husband. He found out about the situation and of his own volition, he went. And once he decided to go, you would not have been able to stop him."

"But he did leave in that craft for Mars that the gatherers brought." Abigail considered it. "And he did kill them."

"And you did not ask them to come here either. Those people came here of their own accord. They made their own choices." He gestured at the black mark. "And they paid for those choices. As they should have; because it was their choice to make. Not you."

Abigail took several breaths to compose herself. "I suppose that is true." She looked up again. "He will not hurt anyone up there."

"Because he promised you he wouldn't?"

Abigail nodded. "Yes. And I take him at his word. And when he comes back, I will ask him if he harmed anyone in saving Gideon. If he did, I will ask him to leave myself."

"Abigail, you don't have to do that. And in any case, as a leader of the town, that is my decision to make. I don't think I even need the council's approval."

"Then you will make it at my suggestion." Abigail said. "Now let us get this cloth back to town. Before these clouds get any darker."

Eli smiled. "If it is indeed water proof, we can unfold it and just walk under it."

Abigial laughed. "That would be a good test."

"And surely a sight as we walk back into town."

Thunder in the distance made them pick up the rolled-up cloth and make their way quickly to town.

They beat a torrential rain by less than half an hour.

Ten

Hugh looked at his map again. The main, interior entrance to the Rollins home was just ahead of him.

When he got there, he stopped to look at the door. He wasn't sure what his plan was once he got inside. If Isaac was correct, the house should have been empty except for whatever servants worked there. Since the Rollins were rich, Hugh expected at least one or two people to be there. From what he already knew about Martians, he expected them to be Earthlings of some sort. With a relegated sigh, he reached into his pocket and pulled out the small FOB that was clipped into the glove of his space suit- it was what let him open the outer door. He raised it to the lighted disk beside the door.

"Hey you!" A voice said.

Hugh ignored it.

"Hey!" Came even louder.

Hugh turned to look. There was a very large man wearing what was obviously some sort of uniform walking brisky toward him. It wasn't quite a jog, but it was definitely at the top end of walking speed.

"Stop right there." The man said.

"Who me?" Hugh asked. He had had many interactions with law enforcement-type people and he had learned over the years that continually asking questions, especially non-confrontational questions, was a good way to find out what the person wanted with him. Before he killed them.

"Yes you. What are you doing?" The man put his hands on his hips as he approached. It made his quick walk look ridiculous.

"Me? Nothing. What is the trouble, officer?" He decided the person was law enforcement instead of a resident of the house he was preparing to break into if his behavior and dress was any indication. Actually, the fingerless gloves were a dead giveaway that he was some sort of hired security that had probably been passed over by actual law enforcement.

The man reached Hugh, towering over him. He stood right in front of Hugh to emphasize the size difference. "There was an unusual airlock access."

"Airlock access?" Hugh asked as he palmed the FOB. "What airlock?" He looked up and down the corridor.

"Airlock Six." The officer scowled at Hugh. "Did you go out?"

"Go out?" Hugh asked. "No; I'm in, officer." He gave a curt nod. "No, I'm definitely inside."

"Don't get funny with me. I don't mean the hallway. The airlock." The officer jerked a thick thumb over his shoulder. "Airlock Six."

"I can't see how that was me." Hugh said, hoping there wasn't video footage of him entering that way. He hadn't noticed cameras, but at this point in time, they could be the size of a molecule for all he knew. He glanced at the man's nametape. "Officer Hazelgrove."

The officer took a step back and looked Hugh up and down. "You sure are mouthy for a primitive." He pointed at Hugh with a finger that was bigger around than Hugh's thumb. "Damned mouthy." His eyes got large. "Where'd you learn to read?"

"Read?" Hugh shrugged. "I honestly don't remember." Now he gave a smirk. "Maybe at primitive school? Wait, a what?" Hugh asked. Then realization hit him; after wearing the clothes for almost four months, he had so gotten used to them he had forgotten that he definitely looked like an Amish person; he was wearing black cloth pants with suspenders to hold them up, a dark blue long-sleeve cloth shirt with wood buttons and a black vest with hook closures. All that was missing was the wide-brimmed straw hat- which he sometimes wore while he was wandering town even though it was nighttime. He fought to keep a smile off his face. "Oh, right."

The officer looked from Hugh to the door and back. "Hey! You're that primitive that the Rollins folks have." He poked Hugh in the chest. "You're supposed to be inside! You're that pet of theirs."

"Pet?" Hugh managed to get the smile off his face; the security officer was about to get him into the Rollins home legally. *Abigail would be so proud*. He thought. "Right. Inside." He reached out his thoughts at the man. "I'm supposed to be inside, I suppose."

The man frowned at Hugh. "Yeah; I suppose I'll just have to put you back inside since Mister and Missus Rollins are out right now."

"Okay, officer." Hugh said. He was sure he was stronger than the man even though he outweighed him by probably close to eighty pounds. But he hoped to get Gideon out without any bloodshed so that Abigail would not feel responsible. He took a step back from the door, concentrating.

The Officer pressed his palm against the glowing disk, it went from white to blue then the door clicked open slightly. He glowered down at Hugh then stepped into the foyer. "Officer Hazelgrove entering the home." He called. "Deimos Front Line Security!"

Hugh remained outside, waiting.

No one responded to Officer Hazelgrove.

"Guess no one is home." Hugh said. "What now?"

"Well get inside then!" The officer smirked. "Welcome home, primitive."

Hugh let a smile grow on his face. "Oh, I was hoping you'd say that, Officer. You don't know how much I enjoy being welcomed into a place." He walked to the entrance of the door then took a big step into the foyer. "Home." He said.

"Smart mouth." The officer grabbed Hugh by the collar. "Let's go."

Hugh let the man drag him into the home. If nothing else, it made sure Officer Hazelgrove stayed near him. While Hugh was walking better in the low gravity, there was no way he could manage to run after anyone- especially a native.

Eleven

"Get in there." The officer said as he shoved Hugh in front of him. "Get going."

Hugh looked around. There were three possible directions to go from the Foyer. Hugh realized the officer expected him to know where to go. He craned his neck around. "I don't know where my cage is."

"What? How can you not know that?"

"They put me in it and I stay there." Hugh shrugged. "I've never been out."

"You're out right now." The officer narrowed his eyes at Hugh. "Smart mouth. If they didn't pay good money for you, I'd knock your smart teeth right out of your smart mouth." He shoved Hugh down the left hallway.

"I don't think this is right." Hugh said as he peered into the first door- a large bedroom. "Let's try the middle one, officer."

The officer grabbed Hugh by the collar and dragged him back to the foyer, Hugh's heels skidding on the polished stone floor the whole way. When they got there, the officer picked Hugh up and put him back on his feet. "Go that way." He pointed at the middle hatchway.

"Yes, officer." Hugh said. He still hadn't run into any other people and hoped the entire residence was empty. If it was, he would have to thank Isaac for his idea when he got back to the ship. Casually he looked down at his watch; thirty minutes had already gone by.

"You in a hurry or something?" The officer said when he saw Hugh look at his watch. He shoved Hugh through a short hallway into a monstrous-sized living area. The ceiling was all glass, giving a panorama of the sky and Mars- when it was overhead, which it currently was.

Hugh looked up at the red planet.

"Never thought you'd be in space, did ya, primitive?" The officer said as he shoved Hugh farther into the room.

"Honestly, no." Hugh said. "I really never thought it would happen." He turned and smiled at the man. "Hey! That's the most honest thing I've said in about half an hour."

"Smart mouth!" The officer punched Hugh in the chest, sending him flying over the back of the couch ten feet away. Thanks to the lower gravity, Hugh landed softly, bounced twice and skidded to a stop against a wall. "Man, I'd love to pound on you for an hour."

Hugh looked up. There was a large glass wall above him. He worked himself to his feet. The glass wall extended ten feet in either direction and seemed to be about ten feet deep as well. There was a bed on one end with a very small wardrobe. Behind the bed was a sink and a very low wall. Hugh realized that the wall was high enough that when the person sat on the toilet behind it, they were only covered from the waist down. It was the ultimate humiliation. On the other end was a small table and one chair. There was a Japanese man sitting in the chair. Hugh's eyes got large. Not because it was a Japanese man; he had seen and interacted with people from the Orient many, many times. It was the fact that the man was wearing a bright red silk robe with blue piping. And he had Samurai face paint on. He even had a bright red feather headdress. All that was missing was the armor. "What in the world?" Hugh said as he looked at the man.

"Damn it all." The Japanese man scowled. "Another Amish? I might just kill myself after all."

"Quiet down, primitive!" The officer said. "No one wants to hear you say anything. And don't go killing yourself until your owners are back. They've been looking forward to it."

"What?" Hugh said again. "Kill yourself?"

"They sit and goad me into committing Seppuku." The Japanese man explained.

"Seppuku?" Hugh said. "Oh right; Hara-kiri."

The Japanese man growled.

"Both of you just shut up." The officer snapped. He marched over and grabbed Hugh by the collar and dragged him to the other side of the room. There was an identical glass cage not twenty feet away. Between them were several couches. Ostensibly for viewing the two cages.

Hugh looked at the cell. There was a man dressed very, very similarly to Hugh sitting on the edge of the bed. He had his head down.

"What the hell is going on?" The officer said when he also spied the Amish man. "There's a second one?" He clapped his hands together. "Oh, that'll be fun when you two go at it. Maybe I can get an invite."

Hugh looked at the officer. "An invite?"

"Yeah. For when you get at each other's throats." He held up a meaty finger. "Then there'll just be one Amish primitive again."

Hugh looked at the man in the cage. "Gideon?" He said softly.

The man didn't raise his head.

"Gideon." Hugh said louder. He glanced at the officer then back at Gideon. "Abigail sends her regards."

"Not her again," the Japanese man scowled. "Anything but that."

The man on the bed shot to his feet. "Abigail!" He moved to the glass and pressed his hands against it and looked around the room, completely ignoring Hugh. "Abigail?"

"Gideon." Hugh said. "Over here."

Gideon looked at Hugh. "Who are you?"

"I'm a friend of Abigail." Hugh smirked. "A good friend."

"Oh, this might get interesting." The Japanese man said lewdly.

Hugh looked at him. "Sonna koto nai." He said in Japanese. It was a casual, friendly phrase used to express skepticism or to say 'that's not true'. Hugh had spent quite a lot of time in 'little Chinas' and 'little Tokyos' because they tended to be in the seedier part of towns. Opium dens were lousy with people who could disappear and no one would ask questions.

The Japanese man's eyes got large. "Nani?" he replied in Japanese. (What?)

Hugh turned back to Gideon. "So anyway, Abigail says she misses you."

"Look who's a chatterbox all of a sudden? Primitive smart mouth." The officer grabbed Hugh by the back of the neck. "Shut up until you are inside." He held Hugh to the side and pressed his palm against the glowing disk on the front of the glass cage. He held his hand there for several seconds.

"Is it not working?" Hugh asked. "It doesn't look like it's working to me."

"It's a safety feature; it takes ten seconds for the door to open, stupid." The officer said. True to his word, after ten seconds, a door opened in the clear wall of the cage. He pushed it open and shoved Hugh in before he realized what was happening. As Hugh skidded to a stop in the low gravity, he turned and tried to run at the door, feet skidding on the ground. The officer pulled the door shut. "Not so smart mouth now are ya!" He gave a curt nod, then marched out of the house.

"There you go, Abigail. Someone I didn't kill." Hugh said.

"You keep saying her name." Gideon said. "How do you know Abigail, brother?"

"I swear to you, if you don't stop talking about her, I will kill you both!" The Japanese man shouted. "Both of you!"

Hugh ignored the man and looked at Gideon. "I was in town and she told me you had been captured. So I came to bring you home."

"But…" Gideon looked around the cell. "How?"

Hugh walked over to the glowing disk and held the FOB against it. He looked at Gideon and winked at him. "Like this."

After about ten seconds, the round disk made a flat double beep sound.

"Oh, wait." Hugh turned the FOB around in his hand and pressed it against the disk again. "Backwards."

After another ten seconds, the disk made the same sound.

"I guess it only works from the outside." Hugh remarked. "Another safety feature." He looked at his watch. "When does anyone get home?"

"No one will be home for three more hours." Gideon said. "If Cy was around, she'd already be here. But she has been gone for a few days now." He considered that. "It has actually been a couple of weeks even. And Ferrule, her husband won't be home for three hours. No one else is here, I'm pretty sure."

Hugh looked at his watch; it was eleven o'clock. "Well, hell." He said.

"I am sorry; they have a schedule." Gideon said.

Twelve

Eli moved to the chair in front of the long table and sat. It had been pulled back from the table so that the person sitting there could look at most everyone without having to turn their head completely from one side to the other. That person at the moment was Eli. "Brothers." He said with a smile to the eight men sitting on the other side of the table. "I hope all is well with you."

"We are all well." The man sitting near the center of the table said. "What we want to ensure is that we and the town continue to be well."

Nods from the other eight men let Eli know that everyone was of one accord. "Then it is good we are speaking because that is what I want also." He smiled again. "So…" His voice trailed off.

The man smirked. "I imagine you have a well-prepared speech, Eli."

Eli blinked. "Oh, actually I don't." He replied. "I wasn't really expecting any sort of inquiry; aren't we just talking?" He looked down at the floor around his chair that was sitting far in front of the table all alone. "I thought there would be food and drinks, and lively conversation at a table. That however does not seem to be the case, Brother Iddo."

"Are you making fun of the situation, Brother Eli?" Iddo asked.

"No." Eli shook his head. "Mainly because I did not realize there *was* a situation." He brought his hands up plaintively. "I thought we were here to discuss how we can continue to support and guide a lost sheep." He paused. "A very lost sheep. Even more so than the nameless prodigal son." He nodded. "It is a blessing that we are in a position to help him."

"Unlike that wayward man, this one kills people, Eli." The man to the left of Iddo said. "How can we condone murder?"

"That is breaking a commandment, Brother Eli." Iddo added. "The sixth."

"We cannot condone it of course, Brother Freeman." Eli said. "Which is what we need to emphasize with Hugh. We cannot and will not condone the killing of others."

"On that we agree then." Freeman said. "Which is why we believe that this person…"

"Hugh." Eli interrupted.

"Hugh." Freeman continued. "Should be asked to leave town." He shifted in his chair. "And I hope he would do so peacefully."

"There is no reason to think he would leave in any other way." Eli said. "Except of course with being hurt and disillusioned."

"He is a killer." Freeman said. "It is all that he knows. He is very much like that other; Benfleet."

"The two were only alike in ailment." Eli said. "In fact, when they met, Benfleet attacked Hugh."

"And Hugh killed him." Iddo said.

"In self-defense; he was infected with the madness. Rabies, Hugh called it. There was no reasoning with him." Eli said. "Sister Abigail explained to me that Benfleet wanted to eat Hugh in an attempt to cure his illness and…"

"Sister Abigail." Iddo interjected. "That is another concern."

"How is Sister Abigail a concern?" Eli asked.

"She consorts with him… Hugh. And visits his home late in the evenings. Late in the evenings with no escort I might add." Iddo shook his head. "Quite improper for a married woman, I should say."

"Are you snooping on citizens of the town, Iddo?"

"I am not." Iddo shook his head. "That is merely what I have been told."

"So now it is hearsay." Eli tut-tutted as he crossed his legs. "My, my. And if that report is actually mistaken then you are bearing false witness against a neighbor. That is commandment number nine, brother Iddo."

"What?" Brother Iddo exclaimed. "Why I…"

"That is not the case at all. You are compromised in your decision making, Eli." Freeman said as he put his hand on Iddo's shoulder to calm him. "Because you are too close to the problem."

"The problem, as I see it." Eli stood. "Is that you would rather turn your back on one of God's children because apparently it would be hard work to try and reach him." He shook his head. "And definitely against our Richtlinien für die Arbeit." He said, referring to the Amish rules that were guidelines that dictated every aspect of Amish life. He put his hands on his hips. "Lazy is what that is."

Freeman's eyes -as well as the eyes of several other men- got large; laziness was a very serious insult. "Now see here!" Freeman snapped.

Nonplussed, Eli pressed on: "Especially since Hugh seems to be aware of a large portion of the Bible; he can quote a great many passages." He shrugged. "That means the words are within him; it is just a matter of giving them weight so he feels them in his heart." Eli turned and headed toward the door. "Apparently *that* yoke is too heavy for you, brothers." He opened the door. "Fortunately, the yoke I carry is easy and my burden is light. So, I have plenty of strength to deal with the likes of Hugh." He stepped through the door. "Good evening to you my Brothers." He closed it softly. Then he leaned against it from the outside.

The men inside sat silent staring at the closed door.

"You were not in there long." Abigail said.

Eli rubbed his face with his hands. "Oh, I should have been, Sister." He looked at her. "I have gone out on a shaky limb for Hugh. A dangerously shaky limb."

"What did you say?"

Eli pushed himself off the door and started walking.

Abigail fell in step beside him. "What did you say?" She asked again.

"I told them they were too lazy to try and reach Hugh."

Abigail's hands went to her mouth. "Eli!"

"And I quoted Matthew chapter 11, verse 28 to them and told them that it meant that I had the strength to spare to deal with Hugh while they did not."

"Oh Eli." Abigail shook her head. "You are going to be shunned."

"Shunned for butting heads with a bunch of stubborn mules?" Eli shook his head. "No, that won't happen." He frowned. "Oh dear."

"What? What else? There is more?"

"I was going to mention to them that they can't actually kick Hugh out of town." He chuckled. "Because he doesn't actually live in town; his home is outside the limits of our town."

"I'm glad you weren't able to tell them that. It's probably bad enough as it is." Abigail said. "The fact that they even brough you in to speak to you was bad enough."

"Indeed; speaking *to* me was bad enough. They should have been speaking *with* me. We should have been speaking *together*. With one another. Of one accord."

"You can't stand against the city council like this. They will put their efforts against you, Eli. There will be a formal inquiry even. You should have shown them patience and understanding."

"Patience and understanding?" Eli smiled at her. "Sister Abigail, they might speak to you next. So it is good you suggest patience and understanding. Bear that in mind, if you would."

"Me? Why?"

"Because you consort with Hugh." He narrowed his eyes and pointed a finger at her. He changed his voice to sound like Brother Iddo, "And you go to his cabin late at night *with no escort*. A married woman no less! Highly improper behavior." He waggled his finger as his voice returned to normal. "Highly improper."

"*What?*" Abigail skidded to a stop. "If they believe I have acted inappropriately I need to speak to them at once!" She started to turn.

Eli grabbed her by the elbow. "Now, Sister. It is late; why don't we wait until tomorrow before any more words are spoken." He pointed ahead again. "Let us get some sleep and tomorrow in the calm warmth of the day, we can both speak to Brothers Iddo and Freeman together. With calm minds."

"I am not sure if my mind will be calm even then." Abigail said. "To think I would be involved with Hugh when I have a husband. Oh!" She shook her head. "And!" Her voice rose. "Hugh is at this very minute rescuing that self-same husband they claim I am being unfaithful to, to bring him back home to me! Why I…" She pulled against his hand.

"Abigail, please." Eli looked around. He was sure that if she lost her temper, word of that would make it back to the two men. "*Calm down.* Tomorrow we will talk with them."

"Oh!" Abigail said angrily. "I will speak to them now."

"No Sister Abigail, we will speak *with* them. With them tomorrow. Let us get some sleep. I am sure that Hugh has everything under control and will be back soon enough with Gideon." He smiled. "And young Isaac. Then all will be well."

"Yes." Abigail shoved her hands in the pockets of her apron. "You are right. Tomorrow we will speak to them."

"With." Reminded Eli.

Abigail sighed. "Yes, we will speak with them."

"Calmly." Eli added. "And *respectfully*."

Abigail tilted her head at him. "Why Brother Eli, that is the only way I speak to anyone. How could you suggest otherwise?"

"Obviously I couldn't." Eli nodded with a smile.

The pair walked to Abigail's home in silence. After she was safely inside, Eli walked to his home. He wanted to at least let his wife know what had transpired so she would be prepared if any of the other women broached the subject of Hugh in the morning.

Thirteen

"Three hours?" Hugh frowned. "Damn it all." He examined the glass walls; they seemed to be an inch thick and there were no seams anywhere. "Wait, how are they able to hear us from inside here?"

"Hey you!" The Japanese man shouted.

Gideon looked at the Japanese man.

"How can they hear us?" Hugh asked again.

"There's a vent over there." Gideon pointed. There was a series of one-inch high, foot-long slits in the glass arranged in a neat square on the far side of the front wall.

"So how do they suck the air out of this box with holes in it like that?"

"Hey!" The Japanese man shouted again.

"The vent goes away, like the door does. Then they suck out the air." Gideon said. "I don't know how it works."

"A vent, huh?" Hugh thought back to Benfleet and how he turned into a mist as he looked at the vent. "Oh boy."

"Hey you!"

Hugh looked at the man. "What's your name?"

"Hinata." The man replied.

"I am sorry; what is it, Hinata-san?" Hugh said, adding the Japanese honorific to his name. He was well aware of the honor system within the Japanese culture and obviously with how the man was dressed, that remained even after all the time that had passed.

"Was this your plan for escape?" Hinata crossed his arms. "Hah!"

"No, this wasn't *my plan for escape.* Obviously." Hugh snapped at the man. "Can't you cut your way out?"

"This is devil glass; my blade doesn't even scratch it." Hinata replied.

"Great. Devil glass." He tapped his headpiece. "Isaac, can you hear me?"

As he expected, he got no reply.

"Hey you!" Hinata shouted.

Hugh ignored him.

"HEY YOU!" Hinata shouted.

"What is it, Hinata?" Hugh said.

"What is your plan now?"

"Well, until someone opens this door from the outside, we're stuck." Hugh said. "There might be a way, but it's something I've never tried before." He looked at the vent again. "And honestly, it scares me a bit." He looked around his cage. "Oh man. No other openings?"

Gideon shook his head. "No. None. You can't even see the door until they open it." He gestured to where the door had been. It was indeed invisible as if it had melted back into the glass.

"No one is here for three hours?" Hugh said. "Not even servants?"

"Servants?" Gideon asked.

"Yeah, these people are rich. I'm sure they don't make their own food or clean their own house."

"Oh. Those. They come out when they are needed. Otherwise, they just stay in the cupboard."

"The cupboard?" Hugh said. "Oh, wait. These are mechanical things, right?"

Gideon nodded. "And they will talk to the others but not us. So you can't ask them for help."

"Okay. I'm going to try something I saw only once and don't even understand how it works, so I need you to both be quiet. Really quiet." Hugh said. "I need quiet, Hinata; got it?"

Gideon took a step back. "What are you going to do?" He asked worriedly.

"Why don't you go sit down on the bed?" Hugh moved to the vent. "And just try to stay calm."

"Okay, I guess." Gideon looked at Hinata who just shrugged, then he went and sat on his bed. He put his head down into his hands and sighed.

Hinata continued to watch with interest.

"Okay. Here goes nothing." Hugh closed his eyes and placed his hand on the vent. He began to think of nothingness. Nothingness in his legs and feet. Nothingness in his body and arms. His clothes were nothing as well. Nothingness. Nothingness Nothingness Nothingness.

The Japanese man leapt to his feet. "Odoroki!" He screamed. (An expression of surprise)

Hugh opened his eyes and looked down; he was all still there. "What? What is it? I said to keep quiet!"

"Devil!" Hinata pointed at Hugh and shouted. "You are a devil! A DEVIL!"

"What the hell is all this noise out here?" A man said as he stepped out from a side hallway that led to the sleeping area. "My head is pounding and you're making a racket. I swear I'm going to pump all the air out and leave it out!" He rubbed his head. "Stupid primitives!"

Hugh looked at the interloper. He seemed to be about thirty, tall and thin like the others he had seen. Except the security guard, of course. "No one here? So who the hell is that?" Hugh asked Gideon as the man stumbled into the room.

Fourteen

"Daniel." Hinata said to Hugh without looking at him. "He is the son. I did not know he was here."

"Neither did I." Gideon said.

"Will you all just SHUT UP!" Daniel said. "I'm not going to say it again." He looked at Hinata. "Still alive, you stupid animal?"

Hinata just looked away.

"And you…" Daniel looked at Gideon's cage. "Why…" his voice trailed off when he saw Hugh. He rubbed his eyes. "Now there's two of you? What the hell?"

Hugh moved to the glass. "Officer Hazelgrove put me in here by mistake." He said as he pressed his palms on the glass. "It was a mistake." He suggested.

"Why are you even in here?" Daniel asked. He rubbed his temples again. "A mistake?"

"The ship… your mother's ship returned." Hugh lied. "She wasn't able to find the girl so she brought me instead." He thought back to the map Cynthia had given him. "She brought me back for the Leopolds."

He said, referring to one of the other families in the complex. "But Officer Hazelgrove brought me here by accident. *An accident you can fix.*"

"I can see how that was an accident." Daniel said. "We were supposed to get the girl." He seemed to come out of his fog. "Mom? Where's Mom?"

"She is on the ship still. She said she had some things to take care of before coming inside." Hugh tried as he continued to concentrate on Daniel. "*Let's get me moved before she comes back from…*"

"Probably having last-minute sex." Daniel said.

"What?" Hugh's concentration broke because the comment caught him off guard both for being a crass thing for a son to say about his mother, and because from what he saw, no one on the ship seemed to like anyone else at all. He concentrated on Daniel again. "So, you should walk me down to the Leopold's home." Hugh said. "*Open the door and take me there.*" He concentrated hard on Daniel. People who were drunk, hung over, or otherwise impaired were much easier to manipulate. "We can walk there together. I'm no trouble at all."

Daniel rubbed his head. "Yeah, we can walk down there together. You people are no trouble. Not like this one." He gestured at Hinata. "Yeah; I'll just walk you down."

Hugh nodded. "*Let's go now* so I can be a surprise for the Leopolds when they get back later today."

Daniel nodded as he stumbled forward. He pulled a FOB from his pocket and pressed it against the glowing disk.

Hinata quickly moved to the side of his cage so he could see the glowing disk.

After what seemed to be a long ten seconds, a door appeared in the glass and it clicked open.

"Okay, let's go." Daniel said as he yawned.

Hugh stepped out of the cage. He looked over at Gideon; he still had his head down. He looked across the room- Hinata wouldn't look at him.

"Come on, I don't have all day." Daniel said as he gestured at the front door. "Let's go."

Hugh took two steps toward Daniel and punched him in the face, knocking him back onto the couch, unconscious. He looked at his watch. Forty-five minutes. "Brother Gideon, how about we go home?"

"What? How?" Gideon looked up at Mars. "How?"

"Earth is that way." Hugh pointed across the room. "We're going that way." He pointed at Mars, "But we will be making a stop on Mars on the way." He looked at Hinata. "Hinata-san."

Hinata wouldn't look at him. "What is it, devil?"

"I'm not a devil." He took a step towards Hinata's cell then looked back. Gideon was still inside his. "Gideon; get out of there in case that door closes automatically. Come sit out here."

Gideon nodded as he left the cage and sat in an overstuffed chair.

As Hugh approached Hinata's cell, he took several steps back and put his hand on his katana's hilt.

"Calm down, Hinata. Let me explain."

"You are going to explain how you are not a devil?" Hinata said. "Hah!"

"Listen Hinata. I don't want Gideon to know but I'll tell you, okay?" He said in a low voice.

"Tell me what, devil?"

"Wait; you saw me disappear? It was working?" Realization hit Hugh. "That's great!"

"Your hand became mist. A grey devil mist."

Hugh nodded. "That's great." He looked at Hinata. "Listen, I'm not a devil; I'm a… Kyūketsuki." He had heard many Japanese men shout that right before he attacked them.

"Huh! A sucking devil. So I am right then." Hinata still wouldn't move near the glass. "You are here to kill us both."

"I am here to *rescue him*. And since you are here, you as well." Hugh said. He looked at his watch then the door. "But we have to go." He looked at Hinata. "I give you my word, I will get you back to Earth. I have promised his wife that I would do that for him, and that is what I am going to do. And you can go as well."

"Huh." Hinata said. "The word of a devil."

"The word of a devil is still a promise." Hugh smiled. "Or would you rather just remain here?"

"Hah!" Hinata smiled as well. "You devils are tricksters indeed. Fine I will go."

"Great." Hugh put the FOB onto the glowing disk and waited. When the door clicked open he beckoned for Hinata. "Get out here."

"What is your name, devil?"

"Hugh. My name is Hugh."

"Hugh-san, I will go with you and hold you to your word." Hinata said. "I am a formidable ally and equally so as an enemy."

Hugh smiled. "Well, having a Samurai on our side would be formidable indeed."

Hinata leveled his eyes at Hugh. "Do you mock me?"

"I do not." Hugh said seriously. "And I will take you with us, Hinata. Back to Earth. On my honor."

Hinata looked up. "But first to Mars?"

Hugh nodded. "Yes, I need to stop there first. But then we go to Earth."

"How?" Hinata asked.

"I have a ship. Waiting across the valley." Hugh looked at his watch. "We have just over an hour to make it there."

"Fine! But I must change!" Hinata said as he moved quickly to the bathroom area of his cage. He yanked off the feather headdress as he went and tossed it aside.

"Well make it quick. I don't want to be here when anyone else happens by." Hugh said. He smirked. "Good old Isaac."

"Wait, you have young Isaac with you?" Gideon said as he raised his head- it seemed to be his default position.

Hugh nodded. "He's minding the ship while I came looking for you." He walked over to Gideon and put his hand on his shoulder. "He's been a great help."

"I do not understand at all. How..." Gideon gestured up and down at Hugh. "How you could be piloting a ship."

Hugh ran his hands down his clothes. "Brother Gideon, I might be dressed like I am Amish but I am not. I was passing by when..." He waved a hand, "It's a long story I can tell you later." He looked at Hinata's cage. "Hinata. Hurry it up!"

"I am washing my face. I will not be rescued painted like a clown!"

"So why do you wear it then?"

"You think I have a choice?" Hinata said. "There is no choice!"

Hugh looked at Gideon. "No choice?"

Gideon shook his head solemnly. "No. They tell you to do something and if you don't, they slowly pump out the air until you agree or pass out. Then they pump air in until you wake up and it starts all over again. There really isn't any choice."

"Man, I'm really not liking these people." Hugh scowled. "At all." He looked across the room again. "Hinata!"

"Do not call me like I am a dog!" Hinata shouted back. "I will come when I am ready and you will be *glad* for it!"

Hugh smiled. "Man, I'm really starting to like him. Perpetually pissed off. That's my kind of attitude. Isaac is going to get fired as my sidekick."

Gideon lowered his voice. "He is a *very* angry man. They killed his entire village when they took him. You need to be careful."

"Oh." Hugh said looking back toward Hinata's cage. "Wow."

Hinata stepped into view. He was wearing black corduroy pants and a loose fitting grey knitted sweater. It was a stark contrast from the brightly colored outfit he had on before. He also had a full length, 30-inch katana strapped to his hip on one side and a shorter 19-inch long wakizashi on the other. "I am ready."

"Formidable ally indeed." Hugh said. "Welcome aboard."

Hinata looked at the glass wall. "Let us go, Hugh-san." He stepped out of the cage with a flourish. "Ahhh." He said. "Now it finally begins."

"Your freedom?" Hugh asked.

"*Revenge.*"

"Oh boy." Hugh said. "Okay, let's get out of here quietly. The last thing we need is the entire complex coming after us." He looked at Daniel; he was still breathing. "Good."

"How will we get to this ship?" Gideon said. "There is no air out there."

"There are suits we will put on. Once we get outside, I will contact the ship and Isaac there will guide us to it because it is dark outside right now."

Gideon nodded. "I will trust your judgement on this, Brother Hugh."

"Great." Hugh gave another nod, then moved across the living area toward the front door. "Stay behind me."

"But you are unarmed, Hugh-san." Hinata said. "Perhaps I should lead the way." He crossed his arms and put his hands on both hilts. "I will defend us all."

"You don't know where we're going and I can handle myself." Hugh replied.

"Fine, I will do as you say, Hugh-san." Hinata said with a frown. "Lead the way."

Fifteen

Eli walked up to Amos; the young man was replacing a fence railing on one of the town's large paddocks for horses. "Brother Amos," he called when he was close.

Amos turned and smiled. "Brother Eli. How goes your day?"

"It is going all on its own, it seems." Eli said with a frown.

"Towards sunset?" Amos laughed. "All of our days do that, I would think."

"It seems that today I am only along for the ride."

"What is the trouble?" Amos balanced his hammer on the newly installed fence rail. "How can I help?"

"I am not sure if you can help with my immediate problems, brother. But there is something you can help with in the short term."

"Name it."

"I need a canoe." Eli said.

"Oh? You and Miriam looking to do some fishing?"

"No." Eli shook his head. "It is for Hugh. When he returns that is."

"Hugh will be doing some fishing." Amos nodded. "He will need a good restful day of fishing after he returns." He cocked his head to the side. "Or I suppose a restful night of fishing in his case. Right?"

Eli laughed. "Right." He became serious. "But it will be more as a… leaving town present."

"Hugh is leaving town?"

Eli sighed. "Well, I have spoken with the elders." He frowned. "Or more accurately I have been spoken to by the elders about Hugh. They want him gone from town."

Amos lowered his voice. "Because he is a vampire?"

"Well, not specifically because of that."

"That is good, because the way I understand it he has no control over how he is. He is as he is, just like the rest of us, no?"

"True. But they are concerned because he has killed people." Eli raised his hands plaintively. "And they are worried he will do it again."

"He is not the same person who walked into our town those months ago. Not at all." Amos said. "We have spent a lot of time together, you know. Building two other canoes, and several rocking chairs and other pieces of furniture. A lot of time together with nothing but working wood and talking."

Eli nodded. "I have also spent a lot of time with him."

"And Abigail has as well." Amos said, then his eyes got large. "Not inappropriately. That is not what I mean at all."

"Yes, I understand what you mean; he has treated her like a sister."

"She is a big sister the way she pushes him around." Amos chuckled. "In Abigail, Hugh has met his match, I think."

"That is true." Eli laughed as well. "But, the issue is with the council. And what they have decided."

Amos picked up his hammer. "Correct me if I am wrong, Brother Eli, but the council was established to be the sounding board for the town, resolve any issues, and to provide direction and guidance when it is needed."

"That is what it says in the town's charter, yes."

"So the council works for us, we citizens of Anchorage."

"You speak the truth, Amos." Eli said. "Level headed truth as usual."

"And secondly," Amos continued. "They cannot shun Hugh because he is not even of our faith. A hat and vest do not an Amish man make."

Eli laughed out loud. "That is also very true. And poetic as well."

"And thirdly…" Amos pressed on.

"I did not mean to get you upset." Eli interrupted as he put his hand on Amos' shoulder.

"And thirdly," Amos said again, "Hugh does not even live in town so they cannot kick him out of it." He held his arms out wide. "What? Does their power now extend to the edges of the sea? Will the Inuit Grand Governor have to listen to the council of our little town?"

"Amos, please." Eli said. "I was not trying to cause a commotion."

"You have not caused one, Brother Eli." Amos slipped his hammer into his well-worn leather tool belt. "Quite the opposite in fact; you have decidedly prevented one."

"Oh Amos, what are you planning on doing?"

"I will inform Brothers Iddo and Freeman." Amos hesitated. "It is them, is it not?"

"It is." Eli said with a sigh.

"I will inform Brothers Iddo and Freeman that they are stewards of this town and if they are unable to accomplish that one task, I will call for a referendum."

"Oh, Amos. No." Eli looked around. "You can't do that."

"Oh, I can. The charter says anyone can, in fact." Amos smiled wide. "And I'm someone, I'm sure of it."

"You are." Eli said. "You are indeed someone."

"So I will speak to them both, then if necessary I will speak to the townsfolk."

"Most of the townspeople don't even know Hugh, why would they have any reason to vote for him for anything?" Eli asked.

"Oh, Brother you are looking at it the wrong way; the referendum is not to keep Hugh in town."

"No?"

"No." Amos shook his head. "It will be called to select a new council." Amos marched off.

"Amos!" Eli called. "Oh dear."

"And I will speak with the Carpenter's Guild because they are all well aware of what Hugh is." Amos called over his shoulder.

"You've told them what Hugh is?" Eli jogged to catch up with Amos. "*All of them?* Oh, I don't know if telling them was…"

"Oh, I told them nothing; they all know because they have witnessed it with their own eyes, Brother Eli." He glanced at Eli. "Of course, you haven't because you aren't part of the guild."

"With their own eyes?" Eli said worriedly. "Guild? What have they seen with their own eyes?"

"That Hugh is a master carpenter. Canoes, tables, rocking chairs, and something he calls an Adirondak chair that is quite comfortable. That chair alone will provide him the full support of the Carpenter's Guild. That is a hundred fifty-two men voting as one."

"Oh, no, Amos, please." Eli said. "This is a great deal of turmoil."

"Jonas!" Amos called to his friend.

Jonas was unloading fence railings and posts from a wagon; they were adding a small section to the paddock for two new foals. "Amos? Are you done with that repair?"

"I am." Amos said as he approached.

"Excellent. Is Eli here to help?" Jonas smiled. "Many hands make light work."

"They do indeed." Amos said. He patted Eli on the shoulder. "In fact, I was just explaining to Brother Eli how many can even speak with one voice."

"Oh dear." Eli said.

"You can use the post hole digger." Jonas smiled. "It's easy to use." He held the long tool out. "Here."

"No, it's not that." Eli said.

"I beg to differ brother; this is indeed a post hole digger." Jonas grinned. "If one is putting post holes in the ground, this is by far the best tool."

"Brother Eli only came by to tell me we need to come to the aid of a fellow carpenter." Amos said.

Jonas placed the blades of the tool on the ground and leaned on it. "Just say what we need to build. Another fence? A crib? It is always a pleasure to build a crib."

"Amos." Eli pleaded.

"Simpler than that, Brother Jonas. All we have to do is explain to the council how we of the Carpenter Guild will not take lightly having one of our members thrown out of town like an Inuit vagabond."

"What? Who are we speaking of?" Jonas asked. "Inuit Vagabond? Eustis may be rough around the edges, but he is no vagabond." He said, referring to an Inuit trapper that often-visited Anchorage. "And he's no carpenter either, now that I think about it." While Eustis was at times brusk from living alone in the wilderness, he at least tried to be cordial while trading furs and such with the townsfolk. There were in fact several outsiders that passed through town regularly.

"Hugh." Eli said. "The Council wants him to leave town."

"And I want fence posts to dig themselves into the ground." Jonas said. "But that is not going to happen either." He leaned forward. "Have you *sat* in an Adirondak? I now have four on my porch." He held up four fingers. "Four. You must stop by, Brother Eli. Truly!"

"I made one long one like a bench for myself and Rebecca to sit on as the sun goes down." Amos said. "It is a nice relaxation after dinner."

"Once you have children, you will want separate ones for them." Jonas pointed out.

"Indeed." Amos tapped his chin. "Perhaps I can alter…"

"You two need to be serious about this." Eli interrupted. "The issue is that the council believes that Hugh is not a good influence on the town because of his past." He took a breath; both Jonas and Amos knew what Hugh was. "Because of what he is, Hugh has killed people in the past and the council cannot abide by that." He shrugged. "Honestly, I can see their point. Can't you?"

"Yes, of course. Hugh did kill people in the past." Amos said. "And I must confess that in the past, I used to soil my diapers." He patted himself on the chest. "But I am better now."

"Amos, please." Eli said.

"You must also know the truth about me then." Jonas said solemnly. "I used to soil my pants as well. In fact, according to my mother, more than any child in this town. But like my brother here." He put his hand on Amos' shoulder. "I have grown out of that habit."

"Thank goodness." Amos said. "And Hugh has grown out of his." Amos looked at Jonas. "There is a verse about this particular situation, no?"

"Oh yes." Jonas replied. "I believe the verse states 'The old has gone, the new is here!'."

"So it is settled." Amos said. He patted Eli on the shoulder. "Do not worry about this matter anymore. Do want to dig the post holes now?"

"I don't know." Eli said. "I do not want to cause a commotion."

"Digging post holes will cause no commotion." Amos grinned wide.

"You know what I mean, Brother." Eli said.

"Do not worry; there truly is no commotion to cause." Amos said. "And as a fourth point, I would like to point out that Brother Hugh is not even here to defend himself, and *that* is specifically mentioned in the town charter. So nothing will happen until he returns." He nodded at Eli. "And when he returns with Gideon, Abigail will easily bring the other members of her quilting group to aid us humble Carpenter Guild members."

"Abigail?" Jonas said. "Oh, we should start praying for both Iddo and Freeman if they attempt to corral her." He grinned wide. "We warned Gideon about her strong-headedness but he didn't listen and married her anyway."

"Our brave Gideon." Amos said.

"I am not sure if this is helping." Eli said. He looked toward town. "I do hope they return quickly."

Amos nodded. "It is a shame they are not back already so this matter could be resolved now."

"Indeed." Jonas grinned again. "Then we could have young Isaac dig all these post holes. We need two dozen of them you know." He gestured across the area. "Benjamin's mare had twin foals so they are small so we are keeping them apart from the others for a little while."

"Well then I shall leave you meek Carpenter Guild men to your task." Eli said. He dusted off his hands. "While I tend to the animals."

"So no post holes then." Amos said. "I suspected as much." He patted Eli's shoulder. "Perhaps next time."

"Please stop by this evening, Eli," Jonas said. "You and Miriam can sit on the new chairs." He jerked a thumb at his friend. "There is not enough room on Amos' bench for the four of you."

Eli let out a long breath. "We will then. See you at seven thirty."

"Seven thirty is it." Jonas replied. "You will see; everything will work out fine."

"How could it not?" Amos added. "With carpenters on the task?"

Eli didn't even try to respond and walked off.

Sixteen

"We're going to be real pals, you and I." Hugh said as he held up a finger. "But I promised a friend I would not kill anyone on this rescue mission." He gestured at Daniel. "And because I gave my word not to kill him…"

"Yes; you keep your word and honor." Hinata said as he stepped over to Hugh and bowed. "I respect that you honor your word to others. It also means your word to me is true." He straightened and shrugged. "I myself made no such agreement with anyone."

"Well, I can understand that." Began Hugh. "But still, I'd rather not have you…"

Hinata quickly drew his katana and plunged it into the still-unconscious Daniel's chest all the way to the hilt. The thirty-inch blade stuck out the back of the couch.

"Hinata!" Hugh exclaimed.

Hinata twisted the blade back and forth to widen the hole then pulled it out. Blood spilled out of Daniel as he gasped awake for a moment, then fell back dead.

Hinata wiped the blade on the cloth arm of the couch. First one side, then the other, then the back. Then he wiped the blade itself, cutting a deep gouge in the arm.

"What are you doing?"

"I will not sheath my blade while it is bloody." Hinata said matter-of-factly.

"No, not that; I get that. I mean killing Daniel." Hugh gestured at the dead man. "I just finished explaining how I wasn't going to kill anyone."

"He has tormented me since I was sold to this family over two years ago. Gideon has seen it since his first day here. Them cheering for me to kill myself. He got what he deserved." Hinata slid his katana back into its sheath, clacking against the hilt when it was in all the way. "Now I am ready."

Hugh looked at Gideon; he was looking at Daniel wide-eyed. "Gideon? Are you okay?"

"I… I think I am." Gideon said.

"Then let's go." Hugh took him by the arm and pulled him up.

"Are you going to drink…" Hinata began.

"Ah, ah, ah." Hugh said as he brought a finger to his lips. "Shhh." He gestured with his head toward Gideon. "No."

"What?" Gideon asked.

"Nothing." Hugh looked at Hinata. "It's nothing, *right?*"

"Right, Hugh-san." Hinata winked. "Let us continue." He gestured at the door.

"Wait." A thought occurred to him. "You said you were sold to these people two years ago?"

"Yes." Hinata nodded, "that is true."

"Where were you before here?"

"I was on Mars with another family who kept me on display in their garden for six months until they decided to redecorate. Then they sold me."

"Cynthia." Hugh said. "Cynthia?" He called again.

"Who is Cynthia?" Gideon said when no one responded. "There is no one here."

"Okay, this is going to be a strange question. Do the people in this house talk out loud to someone who isn't in the room with them but they get an answer anyway?"

"It is a strange question." Hinata said. "With a strange answer; they do. It is someone named Tabatha. But I have never seen her. In my previous prison it was Terrance that they spoke to but I never saw him either."

Hugh nodded. "Right. That's the name of the house. They talk to the house."

"What?" Hinata said.

"Watch." Hugh raised his voice. "Tabatha, are you online?"

"I am always online." Tabatha answered in a smooth, sultry voice.

"Great. Is there a centralized location where I could buy a primitive?"

"There are several online sites that sell indigenous primitives." Tabatha practically coo'ed. "There is not however, a physical location where one can do that."

"I was not lying when I said I was sold, Hugh." Hinata said tersely.

"I know. I'm just trying to get a handle on something. Tabatha, how many indigenous primitives are there?"

"I do not have a way of knowing that." Tabatha replied.

"Why do you not know?" Hugh asked.

"Indigenous primitives are not regulated by the government so there is no way to calculate how many there are currently within the solar system since there is no registration process."

"Okay, well how many indigenous primitives were sold in the past week, month, and year online?" Hugh asked.

"Last week twenty indigenous primitives were sold. In the past month, fifty-two. In the past year three hundred seventy-five indigenous primitives were sold through four different selling sites, each with a different advertised purpose."

"The purpose?" Hugh got a bad feeling. "What are the advertised purposes for the four sites?"

"Two are for art and décor displays. One is for manual labor. The third is for entertainment."

"Oh man, it is amazing how I can hate these people more each day." Hugh shook his head. "Slaves is what they are, right?"

"The term is accurate," Tabatha said. "However indigenous primitives, or just primitives is the currently socially accepted term."

"Do you see why they all need to die?" Hinata asked. His hand went to his katana again. "My blade is the least they deserve."

"We resolved this problem once before. It can happen again." Hugh said, thinking back to his life leading up to the Civil War in the 1850s and through the Civil Rights movement of the 1960s. "It just takes a while." As far as Hugh was concerned back then, all people were alike; blood was blood.

"My way is very quick." Hinata pointed out.

Hugh scowled. "Tabatha, when does Ferrule Rollins return to the house? Do you know where he is?"

"Ferrule Rollins is on Mars at the moment. He is in his laboratory in the city of Lycus Sulci at the base of Olympus Mons," Tabatha answered. "Do you want to contact him?"

"No." Hugh considered his next question. "Where is Cy Rollins?"

"There has been no communication with Cy Rollins for three weeks. Her last location was in the Northern Hemisphere of Earth. Do you want to contact her?"

"No." Hugh said. "Have there been any alerts on Deimos concerning the Rollins' home?"

"There have not been any alerts concerning the Rollins' home. Would you like to activate one now?"

"No, I do not." Hugh said emphatically. "Are you able to open communication to the Rollins' ship the *Giselle*?"

"Yes. Do you want to contact the *Giselle*? It is currently on Deimos so there is no time delay."

Hugh was glad that the artificial intelligence did not seem to mind that while Cy was unaccounted for on Earth, her ship was back on Deimos. "Yes. Yes I do. Open communication please."

"Communication open." Tabatha purred.

"Isaac?" Hugh said. "Can you hear me?"

"Hugh!" Isaac said nervously. "You only have thirty-five minutes left!"

"Yes, that's why I'm calling. I want to make sure you don't leave without us."

"You found him?"

"Yes." Hugh said. "We are on our way back but we might be a little bit late. I just want you to know we will be coming back so you don't try to leave without us."

"Oh... Okay."

Hugh considered that. "Have you started pre-flight procedures?"

"Well, just in case." Isaac said. "I was worried you know."

"Man, I need a new partner." Hugh said. "Sit still Isaac; we are coming to you. If we are a little late, it is fine; we still have to suit up and walk over to the ship."

"Okay?"

"Do *not* take off!" Hugh said.

"Okay."

"Who is this person, Hugh?" Hinata asked. "Can they be trusted to wait for us?"

"Who was that?" Isaac asked.

"We have a second passenger. It's under control." Hugh said. "See you soon. Tabatha, end communication."

"Who's…" Isaac began to say when the communication ended.

"Alright you two. We are heading out." Hugh looked at Daniel's corpse. "We can't just leave him here like this." He said.

"It is more than he deserves." Hinata said.

"Yes, but when someone comes home, we don't want the first thing they see to be a dead Daniel sprawled out on the couch. I'd rather have them come home, get a drink, and do whatever they do normally and not find him for several hours. Preferably once we are off this rock."

"Ahh, that is a good point Hugh-san."

"Let's move the body back to his room. We'll put him back in bed." Hugh said. "Gideon, wait here while we move him." It was obvious that Gideon did not want anything to do with the body the way he was looking the other way.

"Right." Gideon said. "If you say so."

"Hinata, get his feet and I'll get his arms." Hugh shook his head. "Look at all this blood, this is going to be hard to hide." He scowled. "And you even cut up the couch."

"I am sorry Hugh." Hinata grabbed Daniel's legs. "Ready."

"Gideon, instead of sitting there, go ahead of us and figure out which room he was in. It will have an unmade bed in it."

"How do you know that?"

"I've been hung over before." Hugh said. "Get going; we're right behind you."

Without looking at the body, Gideon moved down the hallway that led to the bedrooms- there were five in all.

Hugh picked up Daniel by his arms. As they went, he left a trail of blood. "Oh man." Hugh said. "That's going to be an issue. Tabatha, send the floor cleaners to the living area. There is a wet cleanup there that leads to the bedrooms." He didn't want to mention the word 'blood' and hoped that the robots didn't care what sort of liquid they were cleaning up- or analyzed it.

"Okay. Sending CleanBots to the living room." Tabatha said.

When they got Daniel back into the room that had an unmade bed, they put him in it and covered him with a sheet and blanket. Hugh rolled him so his face was away from the door since he had taken on a pale color. "There. Now let's get out of here before someone else shows up."

Seventeen

The trio walked back out to the living area. There were two square robots cleaning the floor. They weren't doing anything with the large blood spots on the couch. Hugh jogged over and flipped the pillows over- they were clean on the other side. "There. Let's go." He grabbed a nearby blanket and draped it over the cut arm of the couch. Hugh went to the door and opened it. As he leaned out to look left and right, Gideon bumped into him, knocking him into the hallway. "What are you doing?" He looked back.

Gideon raised his hands plaintively. "Hinata is pushing me, sorry."

"I was told time was of the essence." Hinata said.

"Yes, it is." Hugh rolled his eyes. "Revenge waits for no one."

"Well said, Hugh-san."

Hugh shook his head. "Okay, listen; I want to get out of here quietly." He looked back. "I don't want this to turn into a full-out run back to the ship because there is no way that will work out for us. Understand?"

"I understand." Gideon nodded.

"Not you. Hinata?"

"Yes, I heard you. A quiet exit." Hinata replied.

"Great, keep close." Hugh walked out into the hallway, glad to have followed Isaac's advice and come during the day when everyone seemed to be away. He moved quickly down the hallway toward the airlock he had come in. When he got there, he looked back. Hinata and Gideon had stopped just past the door and were looking out a window. "Hey!" He called.

"Oh! I am sorry." Gideon said. "That is amazing. The sight, that is."

"Yeah, you can look at more sights once we are off this rock." Hugh said. "*Let's go.*" He pressed the button opening the inner door of the airlock. "Get inside."

Gideon shuffled up to the airlock and looked in. "Is it safe?"

"Yes. It's safe." Hugh said. "There are clothes to wear there in that bin. Open it up and put them on. They will be big on you, but will still work." He pointed at another bin. "That one is mine."

"Okay." Gideon said with a smile as he opened the bin.

Hugh looked back. Hinata was stalking toward him, hand on his sword. "Let's go before someone shows up." He said.

Hinata didn't speed up his pace.

When Hinata reached him, Hugh poked him in the chest. "Listen Hinata, I came here to get Gideon. You are only going along because I am allowing it. If you are going to endanger my plans, I will just leave you behind. *Got it?*" He poked him again, this time harder.

Hinata looked where Hugh had poked him then back at Hugh's face. "I understand."

"Do you? *Do you really understand?*" Hugh said. "I could have easily left you back in that cage, grabbed this man and left. I don't know if you do get it."

Hinata let out a long breath. "I am sorry, Kyūketsuki. You are correct; I do owe you for saving me." He gave a curt nod. "I will follow your requests and help when I can." He pointed. "In there?"

"Yes, and don't call me that; my name is Hugh."

"What is a Koo ket suki?" Gideon asked. He hopped as he pulled the pants up to his waist. They were easily six inches too long. "This will work?"

Hugh ignored Gideon's question. "Yes, it only has to seal around your legs, hands, and neck. The rest can just bunch up." Hugh stepped back into the hallway to give Hinata enough room to change as well. "I'll dress once you two are done and I have done up your latches."

"Hey!" Officer Hazelgrove called as he rounded the far corner of the hallway. "What are you doing out here?"

Hugh looked over at the man. He was marching with a very angry look on his face. Once again his hands were on his hips. Hugh smiled. "Who me?"

"Yes, you *loudmouth*! I knew you were the one messing with the airlock!" He reached down and pulled out a long black baton. "Damned primitive causing a ruckus."

Hugh casually looked over at Gideon and Hinata- they were both standing rock still. Gideon had just gotten his arms into the suit and Hinata was still holding his. Both of Hinata's weapons were leaned against the wall. "Ruckus? There's a ruckus?" He said when he looked back at Officer Hazelgrove. "Seems pretty quiet around here to me."

"Get away from that airlock. And I mean NOW!" Officer Hazelgrove roared. When he was within ten feet of Hugh, he raised the baton over his head. "I don't care what you cost!"

Hinata stepped out between Hugh and Officer Hazelgrove. "*You will stop!*" He said.

"The two of you?" Officer Hazelgrove said. "It gets better and better." He skidded to a stop within five feet of Hinata. "I'm going to beat you to a pulp. It's going to take a week of T-Cells to get you back to where you can eat solid food! And I don't care…"

Hinata brought his wakizashi up to his shoulders, the blade pointing at the officer's chest. "You will stop." He said again emphatically. He slid his rear foot backwards, to brace his thrust. "I will not ask again."

"Hinata!" Hugh said. "Damn it all, stop killing people!"

"What? Who's dead?" Officer Hazelgrove asked. He pointed the baton at Hinata. "Drop that stupid sword before I brain you! You stinking little…"

Hugh quickly stepped between the pair and delivered an uppercut to Officer Hazelgrove's chin. His head snapped back sharply and he crumpled to the ground in slow motion. His baton clattering to the metal floor afterwards.

"That was the less bloody way to kill him. Nicely done, Hugh-san." Hinata lowered his sword.

Hugh let out a long breath. "This is getting absurd." He pointed at Gideon. "You get your suit on then help Hinata get his on."

"Okay, Hugh." Gideon looked at the large officer. "He's dead?"

Hugh pointed. "He's still breathing. Now the pair of you get your suits on while I get rid of him."

"You will dispatch him?" Hinata sheathed his sword. "Excellent."

"No! I'm not killing anyone." Hugh looked toward the unconscious man.

"He is vermin." Hinata said. "For the past two years he has goaded me into killing myself. He has also treated Gideon terribly. Put him out there." He jerked a thumb at the outer airlock. "He deserves no better."

"Get dressed." Hugh reached down and picked up Officer Hazelgrove by his belt. Even on Earth he would have been able to pick up a two-hundred eighty-pound man with no trouble; with the reduced gravity, it was a simple task. Once while running from a police car, he had flipped a large sedan end-over-end into its path. He hefted the man to waist high. "I'll be right back."

"That is impressive." Hinata said to Hugh as he walked off. "Truly impressive."

"Let's get dressed." Gideon coaxed. "I see how the boots fit on. Get yours on and I can help you."

"Hai."

Eighteen

Hugh stalked down the hallway. Holding the extra weight of Officer Hazelgrove actually made walking easier. "I should bring you along as ballast." He said to the unconscious man. "Making promises to Amish women; what's become of you Hugh?" He said to himself.

When he reached the Rollin's apartment, he pressed the Officer's hand against the pad. Dutifully the door opened. Before stepping in he looked down the corridor- he could see Hinata sitting on the ground putting on his suit. Since he was shorter than Gideon, it was even bigger on him. With a headshake, he entered the apartment. With Officer Hazelgrove unconscious, the previous invitation into the apartment seemed to have ended and now Hugh had an uneasy feeling as he walked in. *Unfathomable.*

Hugh looked left and right, deciding where to put the man- it needed to be someplace secure or he would have to tie him up. With a smirk, he headed toward the large glass cells. "No better than you deserve." When he got there, the door to Gideon's cage was still open. "Perfect." He put down Officer Hazelgrove and took off his belt. Thankfully there was a normal looking radio on it instead of some sort of futuristic communication device implanted in the man's head. He hid the belt under the sofa cushions but not before crushing the radio first. He then returned and tore the Officer's gloves off. "Won't be needing these either." He held up the one that opened the cell door. "Nice."

Officer Hazelgrove groaned as Hugh put the glove in his back pocket. "Awake already, Officer?" He moved to the groggy man. "I wasn't sure how hard I could hit you and not snap your neck."

Officer Hazelgrove rubbed his head. "What? What are you doing?"

Hugh leaned over him and poked him in the chest. "We are leaving." He tilted his head. "And surprisingly enough, you'll still be alive."

"Wh—what?" The Officer's eyes got large.

Hugh leaned over even more, putting his face right next to the other man's. "If it were up to me, I'd have ripped your throat out." He let his eyes change to red and his fangs pushed down out of his upper gums. "And left you to bleed out."

"What!"

"But it seems you owe your life to an Amish woman, of all things." Hugh straightened. "So here's the deal, Officer Hazelgrove…" He began.

Officer Hazelgrove scowled. "There is no deal, you stinking primitive! Get back in your cell NOW!" He sat up. "Or you'll be sorry."

Hugh picked the man up. "You really have no idea how close to death you are." He growled as he changed entirely. "Killing you means nothing to me. Nothing." He opened his mouth wide, fangs extending completely from his mouth.

"You don't scare me, you stinking Berserker!"

"That just proves how stupid you are." Hugh took a running start at the cage and threw the officer through the open doorway. Hard.

Officer Hazelgrove hit the low wall on the far side of the cell, flipping his feet up. He crashed head and shoulders first into the cabinet on the other side and didn't move.

"You better hope we never meet again." Hugh said. He took the glove from his back pocket and pressed it against the cell. After a long ten seconds the door closed. He looked at the ceiling. "Tabatha, will removing sixty percent of the air in the cell be lethal or just uncomfortable?"

"Removing sixty percent of the air from the cell will cause heart palpitations and confusion from hypoxia but would not be lethal." Tabatha replied seductively.

"Tabatha, remove sixty percent of the air from the cell." Hugh said.

"Complying."

Hugh looked back at the cell, satisfied. *Berserker* he thought as he walked out of the apartment. *So I'm a Berserker to Martians?*

Nineteen

Hugh stepped in front of the airlock. Both Gideon and Hinata were wearing suits. He grabbed his own suit and donned it quickly; he had practiced several times on the ship in case he had to get into it in a hurry. He had it on in a minute. "Take a helmet." Hugh said to Gideon.

"What's a helmet?"

"It protects your head." Hinata wrapped his knuckles on his head.

Hugh looked at the man then realized that there was actually no need for a helmet in anyone's life back in Anchorage so the word would indeed be unknown to anyone there. "It's that round thing that goes over your head like a hat. It lets you breathe while you're outside. And protects your head in case you fall, like Hinata said."

"Oh, okay. Helmet." Gideon took it and examined it. He put it on his head with the visor forward. "I'm ready."

"Just a moment." Hugh stepped in front of Gideon and lifted the helmet slightly. He twisted it to the side. "It latches in place like this, then locks when you turn it forward. See?"

"Oh I see, yes." Gideon smiled. "And this will let me breathe outside?"

"Yes." Hugh took Gideon's hand and brought them up to the visor. "Push this button to turn on the air." He pressed a clear button; it turned green. "And this one lets us talk to each other." He pressed another. It turned blue.

"What do the other buttons do?" Gideon asked.

"We will go over those later. All you need now is air and talking." Hugh turned to look at Hinata.

Hinata had already put his helmet on and locked it. "Ready."

"Nice." Hugh said. He took his helmet and leaned out in the corridor. It was empty. Hugh closed the door and donned his helmet. "Here we go." He said as he pressed a large button beside the outer airlock.

The air pumped out of the area slowly.

"The door is not opening." Hinata gestured at the outer door. "Is it stuck?"

"The air is being pumped out of here first so it isn't lost into space." Hugh explained. "Air is a commodity here in space; they try not to waste it."

"So, there is no air at all outside?"

"None." Hugh said.

"I did not expect you to be upset to see that man die. You a Kyūketsuki; sparing a life?" Hinata asked. "Strange."

"I made a promise." Hugh said.

"What is that?" Gideon said. "What he keeps calling you; Kee-yooket suki?"

"It is a word in Japanese for someone who saves people." Hugh lied. "A rescuer."

"Hah!" Hinata laughed. "Oh, Hugh, the lies that come out of your mouth. Your mother must hide her face in shame."

"I don't remember my mother." Hugh said flatly. "Let's go, let's go." He kicked the door.

When all the air was out of the compartment and the outer door opened.

"Finally!" Hugh said. "This is more drama than I was looking for."

"This is more than drama; this is an epic poem. I will write it myself." Hinata said. "The ballad of the sucking devil rescuer, Kyūketsuki Kyūjo-sha; Hugh-San!"

"Work on it once we're out of here." Hugh took a step out. "Okay, it's kind of hard to stay upright when you walk because you can't see your feet." He took a little hop. "But if you skip, you can make pretty good time. Got it?"

"I think so." Gideon said even though he didn't understand.

"Great then let's go." Hugh pointed across the valley. "It's that way about a mile." With that he pushed off with his feet, flying about twenty feet toward the ship. He landed and bounced twice before standing upright. "Like that, okay? Let's go."

Gideon tried to jump the same way but fell over when he landed. "Sorry. I'm sorry."

"By the time you get the hang of it, we'll be back on the ship and you'll never need to do it again." Hugh said.

Gideon jumped once more but not as far, then fell yet again.

Hinata took two skips, bounding twice and landed next to Hugh. "Most perplexing, Hugh-san. But I enjoy it as well."

"Try skipping like Hinata." Hugh suggested.

"What?" Gideon flexed his knees. "Skip what?"

"Skipping. Don't you know what skipping is?" Hugh said. "Hinata understands what it is. How is it you don't?"

"I used to skip with my daughter." Hinata said. "Perhaps he does not have children?"

"That's true, I don't." Gideon said. "I was separated from my wife before we had any."

"Hah!" Hinata said. "I will see you all there then." He took another very long skip- he was clearing close to fifty feet a leap. "Ya hooo!" He cheered as he sailed off.

"You don't know where you are going!" Hugh said. "You're going to get lost you crazy samurai!"

"I am not a samurai." Hinata said. "And I can see the ship when I am high up." He pointed as he arced in the air again. "It is there just a little way. A long sleek white ship?"

"That's it." Hugh said.

Hugh quickly lost sight of Hinata as he made shorter bounds to not lose Gideon. Every time he looked back, Gideon was picking himself off the ground. He was making progress but very slowly. "Are you okay Gideon?"

"I… I think I am now." Gideon responded. "This works."

"Now?" Hugh looked back at Gideon; he was now walking with a shuffle.

"I'll meet you there." Gideon said.

Hugh did one long bound to get back to Gideon then walked up to the man. "Gideon, we need to move quicker or we are going to get caught. Someone is going to find that officer and he knows we were going out that airlock. It won't be that hard to find us and we'll be completely defenseless out here."

"I'm trying, Hugh." Gideon said. He was breathing hard. "I just can't seem to get my feet under me." He stumbled and caught himself with his hands in slow motion. "This is just too strange. Just leave me behind and save Hinata."

"Yeah, Abigail will be fine with that, I'm sure. I didn't bring Gideon, but here's an angry Japanese man instead. Okay?"

"I don't understand why I can walk inside but not outside" Gideon said.

"Next time I'll park closer." Hugh shook his head. "There seems to be more gravity inside because that is what they are used to on Mars." He looked ahead- he could see the outline of the ship. "Tell you what; I'm going to help. A couple of good bounds and we will be there. So let me help you." Hugh offered. He sidled up beside Gideon and put his arm under his and around his back, making Gideon put his arm on Hugh's opposite shoulder. "Ready? We're going to push off together. Ready?"

"Ready."

"Okay, together. *Go.*" Hugh pushed off.

Gideon hesitated and pushed off a moment afterward, putting them into a spin and he lost his grip on Hugh.

"You're going to puncture your suit!" Hugh said. "Or mine!" He tried to pull Gideon around to get a better hold on him but without anything to brace himself against, he wasn't able to. The pair became tangled. Hugh craned his head around; they were heading for a sandy spot between two large rocks. "Hold on to me." He said as they reached the pinnacle of their arc and started down. "Get on my back." Hugh said as they headed for the sandy spot. "Oh man." Hugh tried to get his legs out in front of them to break their fall. Even with only forty percent of the gravity of Earth, the fall from thirty feet could still break bones. Or at least bones in Gideon. "Hang on!" He put his legs out in front of him and flexed his knees. Between the two of them they would have weighed just over four hundred pounds thanks to the added hundred pounds of weight of the two suits. With only forty percent of the gravity of Earth, Hugh was still falling with a hundred sixty-five-pounds of mass. Even though this was ten pounds lighter than he was, it was in a much more cumbersome shape. He tried to think of gliding but it seemed that did not work in space. "Well that's just annoying." He said.

"What?" Gideon tried to look over Hugh's shoulder. "What's annoying? Me?"

"No; just hang on!" He said as the ground came at them quickly. Now it looked like they would be landing very near the large rock on the left. Which thanks to not having any atmosphere to weather it, was a jagged mess. He put his arms out, hoping to keep off the edge of the rock, which was now within their trajectory.

"What are you doing, Hugh?" Hinata said. "Are you coming or not? This infuriating man won't let me inside!"

"I'm in the middle of something!" Hugh shouted as he hit the edge of the large rock with his hand. It tore a hole through the palm of his glove and up to his forearm. He successfully twisted to keep Gideon off the rock, managing to dump him off on the soft ground.

Gideon slid almost twenty feet. "Are you okay?" He said as he stood shakily. "Hugh?"

Hugh grabbed his elbow tightly, trying to keep the air inside his suit. A red light went off on his head's up display, then another. Within a moment, the suit tightened around his lower bicep, stopping the loss of air. "Oh, modern technology." Hugh said. He looked down at his hand- it was already turning a very pale color as it started to freeze. "Get to the ship!" Hugh said as he started that way quickly. "Gideon, get to the ship! Isaac, are you there?"

"Is everything okay?" Isaac asked. "It sounds like everything isn't okay."

"Everything is okay. Open the outer door. We are almost there." Hugh took two bounds and was past Gideon. "Move it Gideon!" He said as he took another bound. It put him at the ship.

"Are you okay? I saw you hit that rock." Hinata said worriedly.

"I'll be fine. I hope." Hugh held up his hand again to look at it through his visor. It was completely grey.

"Is that *frozen*?" Hinata said. "Nantekotta!" (Oh no)

"Yes. But it's all in one piece, which is good news." He turned around. "Gideon!" He shouted just as he stepped into the airlock. Gideon was right in front of him. "Oh. Finally." He pulled him in a little farther then hit the button to close the outer door.

"Wow." Gideon said as he looked around the small space.

Hugh ignored him as he turned around and pressed the icon to open the inner door. Dutifully, air hissed into the small space. After just a few seconds the inner door opened.

"Everyone in. We need to get off this rock." Hugh took off his helmet as he stepped into the open area at the airlock. "Isaac, help Gideon get out of his gear." He gestured. "This is Hinata. Help him too."

Hinata gave a nod. "Isaac. It is good to meet you." He started taking off his helmet.

"And you." Isaac pressed the lock on Gideon's helmet, twisted it to the side and lifted it off. Hugh had made sure he knew how to don and remove an atmosphere suit just in case he had to leave the spaceship. He smiled at Gideon. "It's good to see you Brother Gideon."

"Isaac. It has been a long time." Gideon smiled at the young man. "What an adventure you are on."

"Yes, I really…" Gideon's voice trailed off as he looked at Hinata, eyes wide. "What?"

Hinata looked behind himself. "What?"

"He's an Inuk!" Gideon said. "Why do you have an Inuk with you?"

"A what?" Hinata asked.

"No, no." Hugh said as he tugged down his suit and stepped out of it, being careful with his frozen arm. "He's Japanese. They're totally different."

"He looks like an… an Inuk."

"What is this Inuk.?" Hinata dropped his wakizashi and grasped his katana with two hands, ready to unsheathe it. "What is it you are calling me? Do you dare insult me, a guest here? Tell me!"

"Hinata, calm down." Hugh said. "The Inuit are people that the Amish do not get along with. They look similar… *similar* to the Japanese." He looked at Isaac. "But they are not the same people."

"They aren't?"

"*No.*" Hugh said emphatically. "Technically Inuit are more related to Mongols. If they even exist anymore."

"Ahh, Mongol hoards do indeed still exist." Hinata said. "If the Inuit are like them, then we have a common enemy, Isaac."

"Oh." Gideon looked at the deck. "Then I am sorry for the misunderstanding." He looked up. "I apologize…"

"Hinata." Hinata said. "Hinata Takahashi." He gave a short bow. "And it seems you are also Amish?" He looked between the three men. "My lots have been cast in a most perplexing way."

Isaac perked up. "Yes, I'm Amish. Do you know about us?"

"I have heard about your people at great length." Hinata glanced at Gideon. "Very great length."

"Wonderful!" Isaac said. "Maybe you can tell me about…"

"Great, great." Hugh interrupted. "Now that we're all friends again, Isaac get Gideon out of that suit then go to the first aid console and draw a unit of blood like I showed you. Gideon you help Hinata out of his suit. I'm going to get us off this rock before anyone notices us."

"Oh, was someone hurt?"

"Him." Hinata pointed as Hugh. "His arm is frozen."

"Oh, that will never heal." Gideon said. "And frostbite will kill you. We need to get that arm off as quickly as possible." He leaned in and looked at Hugh's grey hand. "Oh, that is bad. You will lose it up to the elbow for sure, my friend."

"Isaac, get Gideon undressed and then bring me a unit of blood. Hinata you can choose a bunk to sleep on and put your swords there. You won't need them on the ship." When he had first explored the ship, Hugh had gone through the ship's infirmary; it was actually quite extensive with a robot capable of complicated surgeries, setting and casting of breaks, as well as diagnosing ailments. It also had a dozen units of O positive blood. Hugh decided that at times, previous interactions with locals became physical so a sophisticated infirmary had been added to the ship were one of the sleeping births had been. The ship now only had three births.

"Hai." Hinata said.

Isaac looked at Hinata. "What?"

"Just get to your tasks and…"

"Incoming transmission." Cynthia said.

"Who was that?" Gideon asked.

"Here we go." Hugh turned and walked quickly to the cockpit, hoping everyone accomplished their task quickly. Especially Isaac.

Twenty

Gideon looked at Isaac. "Can you control this craft?"

"No." Isaac said. "Why do you ask that?"

"Hugh is hurt. But how are we going to remove his arm if he is the only pilot?" Gideon said. "I remember when Nathaniel lost his arm after a bear attack; he was laid up for over a month and even a year later had not fully recovered. We can't just sit here a month, can we?"

"This ship has an automatic doctor." Isaac said. "Maybe it can help. We have to remove his arm?" Isaac looked forward. "Really?"

"His suit got torn." Gideon frowned. "Because of me. And because it tore, his arm froze."

"No." Hinata shook his head. "I do not believe he will lose his arm."

"What?" Isaac looked at him. "What makes you say that?" He returned to unlatching Gideon's leg connections on the suit.

"He is a Kyūketsuki. They heal quickly."

"A what?" Isaac said as he stood.

"You called him that before and he made light of it." Gideon said. "What is it really?"

Hinata looked toward the cockpit. While Hugh had asked him not to discuss what he was, that secret was going to be in the open for all to see when they all saw his arm healed. "He is something different than us. A creature that can heal." A thought occurred to him. "That is why he asked you to bring him blood. Blood will heal him."

"I don't see how that is possible." Gideon said as he stepped out of the suit. "I have had experience with frost bite and it is not something that heals. Ever."

"He will have to explain it to you. He asked that I do not, and since he has rescued me from my prison I will abide by his request."

"Where is that blood!" Hugh shouted through the ship's internal sound system. "What is taking so long?"

"Take the blood to him, Isaac." Hinata said. "I will join you in a moment once Gideon has helped me with these clothes and I have put my weapons in a room."

"Okay." Isaac said, worriedly as he turned toward the infirmary.

Twenty-One

"Cynthia, who is hailing us?" Hugh said as he eased into the seat. "Another ship?"

"We are being hailed by a Flight Operation technician." Cynthia replied.

"Explain what Flight Operations is." Hugh said, not sure if he was dealing with a small local office that dealt with Deimos, or something larger.

"Flight Operations is a division of the Department of Transportation of Mars. Maurice VanBuren is the head of Flight Operations and reports directly to the Deputy of the Department of Transportation, Ellen Paris. Maurice VanBuren has several agencies and commissions which he…"

"Stop." Hugh said. "So, Flight Operations is contacting us? Is it for the whole Solar System, Mars, or just Deimos?"

"It is Mars Flight Operation, Moons Section contacting us. Is it a sub-office that is responsible for spacecraft on and around Deimos and Phobos." Cynthia said. "Do you want to reply?"

"I suppose I have to." Hugh sighed. "Open communication."

"*Giselle*, this is M-F-O Moons. Do you read?" A voice said.

Hugh took a deep breath to calm himself then responded in his 'pilot voice'. "Roger M-F-O Moons, I read you now. Sorry about that; I was in the head."

"Copy, *Giselle*." The man replied. "What is your status?"

Hugh considered the question; he wasn't sure how to answer it. "Our status?" he repeated. "Uhmm… ship's functions are in the green, crew morale is good. We're critically low on beer. Can you clarify, M-F-O Moons?"

"Why are you laid up in the middle of the Fermi Plain instead of docked at your place of residence?" The man said. His voice seemed to be a little more agitated. "We have a BOLO request for Doctor Rollins from her husband." He added.

"Well, you don't need to Be On the Lookout For Cy anymore; she's here with us, M-F-O Moons. All is okay here. Except for the beer supplies." Hugh hit the mute icon. "Cynthia; Carl, the owner of this ship. What family does he have? Does he have a brother, sister?"

"Carl Nunis has two brothers; Devin and Leroy." Cynthia asked.

"*Giselle*, who am I speaking with?" The man asked on the radio.

"Are either of them on Mars or one of its moons?"

"Devin Nunis is on Phobos. Leroy Nunis' location is currently unknown."

"Where was his last known location?" Hugh asked.

"*Giselle*, do you read?" The man asked.

"Where was Leroy Nunis' last known location?"

"In the Asteroid Belt, near Vesta. He has not opened any communication links in six days."

"*Giselle* do you…"

Hugh tapped the mute button. It went from red to green. "Calm down, MFO; I was getting the last beer. This is Leroy Nunis." Hugh interrupted the man. "I'm traveling with my brother, Carl. He's got me right seating while he deals with a cargo issue. Once it's locked down, we'll be pulling in."

There was a hesitation, ostensibly as the M-F-O technician tried to locate Leroy. After a few seconds he responded: "Roger that, Leroy. We thought you were on Venus."

Hugh smiled; the man was hoping to catch him in a lie. "Negative M-F-O Moons, I was over by Vesta running down a business proposition when my brother asked for some assistance with a primitive. The locals were giving him some trouble." He scowled and let it leak into his voice. "Not that it's any business of M-F-O where the hell I was." He added.

"Understood." The man replied in the same calm demeanor. "Seemed suspicious is all. I was worried the *Giselle* was having mechanical trouble set down where she was."

"The *Giselle* is just grand." Hugh said. "We'll be moving off shortly. *Giselle* out." He closed the communication link. He exhaled loudly and pressed the internal communication button. "Where is that blood!" Hugh shouted. "What is taking so long?" His arm was starting to throb as it thawed.

Twenty-Two

Brother Iddo sat on the bench in front of his house. "So." He said.

"So," Jonas repeated. "All we need to do is wait for Hugh to get back here so this can all be discussed together as a community."

"There is nothing to discuss." Iddo said. "A decision has been made and it will be abided by. And as far as him being part of the community, I think that is going a bit too far."

"Brother Iddo." Jonas looked at Amos who nodded at him. "I believe that being in the council is not good for you. It has made you… uneven."

"Uneven?" Iddo asked.

"Yes; you are unevenly yoked between your personal life and the position. I have never seen you so angry about anything. Even the floods two years ago did not bother you as much as this. It is troubling and needs to stop, I think."

Iddo sat up. "What are you telling me exactly?"

"I am not telling you anything. I am *explaining* to you, Brother Iddo that for your own good, and the good of your household, it would be best that you no longer serve on the council. Which is why I ask for a referendum on your position." Jonas said.

"What?" Iddo stood. "You do not have the authority to do that."

"Brother Iddo, the town charter specifically says anyone can request a referendum if they have just cause. Any citizen of the town. And I believe your anger is just cause to determine if perhaps the position is becoming too much for you." Jonas looked at Amos.

Amos nodded. "Honestly, Brother Iddo, I would not want the position myself; it is a great deal of responsibility that I do not think I would be able to properly handle." He shrugged. "The position is not for everyone; on that we can surely agree."

"Anger? You think I do this out of anger?" Iddo said to Jonas, ignoring Amos completely.

"It seems to be, yes." Amos pressed on. "And keep in mind you would not be the first person to step down from the council. Not even recently. In fact, there were two that have done so in the past year; brothers Stephan Miller and Moses Stoltzfus. For different reasons, of course. And many more before them; it is not a lifelong position, after all."

"Let me ask you three a question and your answer will be my answer on stepping down." Iddo sat.

"Brother Iddo, we are not here to play word games with you." Eli warned.

"I will ask a question," Iddo said again. "And your answer will also be my answer to you."

"Who will answer?" Jonas asked.

"It will be a group question." Iddo crossed his legs. "A consensus; how you answer as a group will also be my own answer."

Eli let out a long sigh. "Fine, Brother Iddo; ask your question."

"And how we answer will be your answer to stepping down?" Jonas smiled. "What if we answer yes?"

"Is this a trick question?" Amos asked. "There isn't mathematics involved is there?"

"Oh, that would definitely leave you out of the discussion, Brother Amos." Jonas said with a wide smile. He winked at Iddo. "No mathematics please, Sir; they do confound my brother."

"You speak the truth, Brother Jonas." Amos also winked at Iddo. "Numbers confuse me sorely."

"Ask your question." Eli said again, now sorry that he had allowed the two younger men to accompany him.

"When the Inuit attack us." Iddo raised a finger, "and that brothers in not a question of 'if'; it is a question of 'when'. *When* the Inuit attack us, will you three be happy to just sit and watch Hugh kill the attackers? Because he most assuredly will kill every single one of them."

"Now wait a moment." Amos said. "I do not see how that is a fair question."

"It is THE question," Iddo said. "You have someone living in our town who does not follow our ways." He gestured at Eli. "And I do understand he is familiar with and has memorized great portions of the Bible. That is not the issue at hand. The issue is when it comes down to it, are you all willing to tolerate Hugh killing others in our defense?" He gestured at Jonas. "And do not tell me brother, that he lives outside of town because I am well aware of where his home is. Word games indeed. Its location makes no difference because he considers this town his home." He pointed skyward. "Otherwise he would not be somewhere up there trying to find Sister Abigail's husband." He shook his head. "I wonder how many have died at his hands in *that* endeavor. And what will Sister Abigail think of herself when she finds out the number."

"Wait a moment here, Brother Iddo, you are muddying the waters." Jonas said seriously.

"I disagree, Brother Jonas." Eli said. "It is indeed a fair question that I have considered myself. However there is precedent that would allow us an answer of 'no'." He hesitated mentioning his discussion about this very issue with Abigail. And how he had prayed the following two days trying to come to a decision on it. "I have actually prayed about this very issue myself." He finally said. "My answer is 'no'."

"How do you figure that, Brother Eli?" Iddo asked. "Blessed are the peacemakers, it is said."

"And we have in the past allowed our dogs to fight the Inuit when they attacked the town." Eli said. "We did not pull them into our houses when they attacked. Dozens of dogs left outside."

"Are you equating Hugh to a dog?" Iddo raised an eyebrow.

"And," Eli continued. "The last time they attacked in earnest- last spring, there were several outsiders in town at the time. Eustis, Tamole, and August were all here and all of them fought against the Inuit." He pointed at Iddo. "And *you* brother said at the time: 'Thank God for these men being here in town at the moment when they were needed the most'. You called it a divine intervention, in fact."

"They are not citizens of town." Iddo pointed out. "They are always just passing through."

"Yet you felt that God had sent them to town precisely when it needed to be defended." Eli said. "The fact that they killed several Inuit to ultimately repel the attackers is just that; a fact. And yet they are still allowed to come and go." Eli said.

"Eustis was here just three months ago." Jonas said. "He came into town, spent a week sleeping in my barn, and then left back into the wilderness after trading pelts for supplies and clothing."

"I dealt with him as well." Amos confirmed. "I traded fixing his sled for some pelts, in fact. No one told me I was forbidden to and it was common knowledge he was at my home; we even had neighbors over for dinner while he was a guest."

"So you see, Brother Iddo?" Eli said. "Not only are we fine with allowing others to fight for us and even send thanks to God when they do, we continue to barter with them, share meals with them, and allow them to sleep under our roofs. Fortuitous, I believe was another word you called it."

"It is a dangerous precedent you are trying to establish," Iddo shook his head. "So we allow this Hugh to remain in town. Someone with extraordinary abilities that we really do not understand. And he will be what, our guard dog? Our mercenary to dole out punishment against those that wrong us?"

"That's not what we are saying," Amos said.

"If you are saying you are accepting the fact that Hugh may kill people in our name, or for our sake." Iddo looked upward. "He probably already has at this point; I should point out."

"You do not know that, Brother Iddo." Eli interrupted. "Abigail made him promise not to kill anyone while trying to find her Gideon."

"Brother Eli," Iddo pleaded. "You are probably not aware because they lived in the north part of town but the very evening Hugh arrived here, a hunting party of seven men went missing. Seven men, never to be seen again." He raised an eyebrow. "You were aware?" He added when Eli looked away.

"Hunting is dangerous work." Eli said uncomfortably since he was well aware of the incident. "But yes, I am aware of it." He was not able to lie to Iddo. "It was tragic to hear."

"All seven, two of which were armed, all were killed." Iddo shook his head. "It is indeed a coincidence that just before this stranger with extraordinary abilities shows up, seven of our citizens go missing. And." He raised a finger. "I also believe that the four gatherers who came here are also dead."

Eli closed his eyes; he and Abigail decided not to speak to the council about the woman's rise from the dead. It had gotten back to them however that the four interlopers were dead. "Yes. Yes, they are."

"They were here to take citizens of town." Amos argued. "Kidnap us."

"Oh, so now you are fine with having people killed who aren't even killing us? What is next? If a trader does not give what you consider a fair price for your labor, do you set Hugh on them as well?"

"That's not what I said at all!" Amos said. He shook his head. "You are confusing me."

"You should all go home and pray about what you want your actions to be." Iddo said. "In the meanwhile, I will continue to work on the council to keep the town moving along a righteous path."

"No, I don't think that ..." Jonas began.

"Let us go, brothers," Eli interrupted. "We have taken too much of Brother Iddo's evening as it is." He stood and moved to the stairs of the porch. "We bid you a good night, Brother Iddo." He tipped his hat at the man. "And we truly appreciate your time and patience."

"And I yours." Iddo pushed himself off his bench. "Have a quiet, restful evening, Brothers."

Eli tugged on Jonas' shirt sleeve when it looked like he wouldn't follow. "Let us go."

The trio walked down the stairs into the darkness.

"Brother Eli," Amos said. "I don't see how you could agree with him that Hugh should leave."

"We didn't agree to that." Eli said. "What we did agree to was that we were not going to use Hugh to fight for us." He patted the young man on the shoulder. "Because ultimately that is the right thing to do."

"I suppose that is true." Amos said. He thought for a moment then smiled wide. "But perhaps with Hugh here we can establish an accord with the Inuit!"

"What?"

"Brother Eli, the issue is that the Inuit come when they want and take what they want. With Hugh here, they would reconsider their actions."

Eli looked at him. "That could be possible. The threat of what Hugh could do to them might be enough to have an assembly with them and discuss the relations between the Inuit and Amish." He nodded. "Yes; that is something I will discuss with the council. If I went as emissary with Hugh accompanying me, they might be inclined to listen."

"That would be a wonderful change if we did not have to worry about coming across any Inuit hunting parties." Jonas said. "To be able to sit down at a fire as friends would be a wonderful change."

"Indeed it would." Eli said, considering it. "That is definitely possible once we are able to speak with them." He smiled at the pair. Hugh had mentioned that he spoke Inuit at dinner once. "That is a lot to think about."

"Let me know Brother Eli." Amos said. "If there is anything that I can do to help."

"And me as well." Jonas said.

"Good night to you both." Eli said. "Enjoy your adiron chairs."

"Adirondak." Amos corrected. "They are named after a mountain range far to the east apparently."

"Adirondak." Eli nodded. "They were comfortable. Perhaps tomorrow evening I will have time to come sit in one again."

"By then we will have made you two." Amos replied. "They are a simple, elegant design."

"Then I will wait for you on my porch." Eli said with a wave. "And tomorrow I will speak with Brother Freeman." He added.

Twenty-Three

Isaac rushed into the cockpit. "Here is the blood. But I don't see how it is going to help."

Hugh took the large plastic sack. It already had a tube and hypodermic needle attached to it. "Why don't you go see if Gideon wants something to eat or drink?" He asked.

"Oh." Isaac looked back into the ship. "I suppose I could do that." He looked at the plastic sack of blood. "I…"

"Go be a good host to Gideon." Hugh said. "He is unfamiliar with the ship and won't know how to prepare food or drink. And I'm sure he would like to talk to someone friendly for a change."

"Oh. Okay." Isaac said, even though he still didn't move.

"You are in the way, young Isaac!" Hinata said as he stepped into the cockpit as well. "Go elsewhere!"

"I don't need you here either." Hugh said with a head shake. "I think it would be better if I were up here alone piloting the ship."

"Really?" Isaac said.

"Really." Hugh affirmed. "Go help Gideon, Isaac."

"Yes!" Hinata grabbed a handful of Isaac's shirt and muscled him around toward the hatch. "Go. Go tend to your Amish friend, young Isaac."

"Hey now!" Isaac said as he was half shoved, half tossed from the small area. "I do not think that is very polite of you Hinata." He looked at Hugh for support. "Hugh?"

"I will speak to him about it," Hugh said. "Isaac go. Hinata sit down so we can discuss manners." He pointed at the copilot seat. "And do not touch anything."

"Hai." Hinata said as he eased into the seat. He peered at the monitors that were giving views of Deimos, Mars, and the dark sky. "Devil magic."

With a huff, Isaac stepped out and pressed the button to close the door.

"Ahh, you are now alone and can drink that blood, Kyūketsuki." Hinata said. "I will not watch you." He focused on the monitor in front of him. "Drink it now."

Hugh looked from the bag of blood to Hinata and back. Now he was self-conscious about drinking it in front of him so he hesitated.

After a long moment Hinata looked over at him. "Hugh-san. You said we need to leave. If you need your arm to pilot this craft, you must drink that now. I would not think less of such an honorable man as you."

"Bottoms up." Hugh said as he unscrewed the port that the IV used and dropped it to the deck. He then began sucking the blood out of the bag.

"Should we have warmed it?" Hinata asked.

Hugh shifted his eyes over to look at Hinata but kept drinking. Within moments, the blood was gone. It tasted strange because it was chilled instead of body temperature, but he could immediately feel the effects of it; the pins and needles feeling in his arm increased. "Oh man!" He said as he screwed the cap back onto the empty bag. "Oh, that hurts!" He dropped the bag beside the chair.

"You feel pain, Kyūketsuki?"

"Stop calling me that." Hugh snapped. "My name is Hugh."

"I do not mean offence Kyū… Hugh." Hinata said. "So now we leave?"

Hugh looked at the camera feeds; Deimos had turned so they were now on the opposite side of from Mars looking into space. A thought occurred to him. "Cynthia. How does flight operations track ships?"

"Mars Flight Operations is able to detect the magnetic signature of ships as they pass by. It is unique for each model ship. They then lock onto the signature and track the ship until they are out of range."

"And our transponder tells them who we are once they are locked on and what; ping us?"

"I do not understand that term." Cynthia said.

"They request identification from the ships onboard system."

"Yes." Cynthia replied.

"So now that we are out of sight of Mars, how do they know we are here?"

"Mars Flight Operations, Moons Section uses the last known location of a ship to track it. Once we are no longer in eclipse, they will once again monitor the ship's position using the last known location to lock onto it again."

"But we can still talk to them?"

"Yes. Communication is relayed system wide."

"Okay." Hugh considered that for a moment. "Cynthia, how long are we in eclipse?"

"Thirty-two minutes."

"Great. Perfect." Hugh said. "Hey, Cynthia; is this a regular ship that we are in?"

"Define regular." Cynthia replied.

"The model ship we are currently in; how many of these ships does that company make? How many of this particular model are there currently in service?" He cringed because often asking more than one question at once caused the AI to give strange answers.

"There are currently two thousand six hundred seventy-nine Voyager model, Planet-Hopper trim package ships built by Nelson-Healey Aerospace Systems Incorporated currently registered. There may be more in operation that are not registered however."

"That's a good number of ships." Hugh said. "Perfect. Cynthia; can you change our transponder to…" He thought for a moment. "Change it to *Knik Anchorage*?"

"I cannot change the transponder of the *Giselle*." Cynthia replied.

"Oh man, I was worried about that. It has to be done at the factory, I'll bet." Hugh said. "Am I right; the factory has to change it?"

"The transponder must be changed manually at the main control board." Cynthia said. "It is a manual function for security reasons so that it cannot be changed remotely."

"Where is the main control board?" Hugh asked.

"It is located amidships in between the infirmary and the galley in the bulkhead marked 0-01 M-C-B."

"Excellent." Hugh looked at Hinata. "Can you read?"

"Of course I can read." Hinata said. "What do you take me for?"

"Oh." Hugh smiled. "I mean can you read *English*."

"No." Hinata shook his head. "I can speak it because of the time I have spent in captivity but I have not been taught to read or write it." He frowned. "Of course, I am an excellent writer and reader in my own tongue."

"Sure, sure, I was just asking." He looked up when he addressed the AI. "Cynthia, what does it take to change the transponder?"

"It is a manual entry on a keypad. Then an MCO-1255 Name Change form must be submitted to Mars Operations within seven days to legally change the name."

"So that..."

"Also," Cynthia continued. "This form must be sent to Nelson-Healy Systems Incorporated on the asteroid Pallas to ensure continued warranty coverage."

"Sure, I'll submit it in writing when we get to Mars." Hugh said. He looked at Hinata and shook his head. "And I'll worry about the warranty later. For now, do you have any issues with us changing the name of the ship?"

"The name of the ship does not affect my operating systems." Cynthia said.

"Great. When does eclipse end?"

"Twenty-seven minutes."

"Cynthia open communication with Mars Flight Operation, Moons Section."

"Communication link is open."

"M-F-O Moons, this is the *Giselle*. Just wanted to let you know we're pulling into the hangar and shutting down for the day." Hugh said. "Our cargo is under control."

"Roger that, Giselle. Thanks for the update." A different technician replied- it was a woman this time. "Glad you're home safe."

"Safe and sound." Hugh said then he pressed the 'end transmission' icon. "Okay, let's get the name of this ship changed." He stood.

"I don't see why the name of the ship is significant." Hinata said. "Why would the…" His voice trailed off as he saw Hugh's healed arm. "Odoroki, your arm!"

Hugh flexed his fingers. "Much better."

"You must know," Hinata began as he stood as well. "Those other two asked me about you. Once they see you are healed, they will have more questions. I honored your request and did not tell them anything but now I think they will be very insistent." He scowled. "They are an insistent and chatty people."

"I will speak to them." Hugh replied. "Let's go. You can get something to eat while I get the name changed."

"Hai." Hinata moved around the copilot chair. "What is a Knik Anchorage?"

Hugh pushed the button opening the hatch. "They're from the town of Anchorage." He gestured into the ship.

"I see. So what is a Knik?"

"After you." Hugh held out his hand gesturing into the back of the ship. "It's the name of the town from a long time ago, then it was shortened to just Anchorage. I can tell you the tale later."

The pair walked into the galley area.

"Are we moving now?" Isaac asked.

"Not yet." Hugh answered. "There's something I need to do first." He looked at Gideon; he was eating a bowl of food. "What'd you give him?"

"Macaroni and the chili mixed together." Isaac said.

"It is better together than individually." Gideon said. "It is still not great, but it is filling."

"Chili-mac; a universal constant." Hugh shrugged. "That is all the food in here is good for; filling your belly." Hugh pointed at Isaac. "Please get Hinata something to eat while I get the ship ready to fly. Cynthia; how long until eclipse ends?"

"Nineteen minutes."

"Oh man." Hugh said. "We need to be underway before that." He looked at the panels along the wall. He had not noticed the small, neatly stenciled numbers on them until now. "There we go. Main Control Board one." He said as he walked to the one with 0-01 MCO on it. He pushed in the grey colored button at the top then pulled the top of the panel away then lifted the bottom tabs out of their slots and picked up the entire panel. He set it on the deck beside the opening. Inside was a mass of wires and circuitry. "Wow, you'd think it would be neater than that after all this time."

Hinata peered over his shoulder. "What is all that?"

"That is what makes the ship work." Hugh examined the wires.

"Devil work." Hinata said with a head shake.

"Probably." Hugh remarked.

"Hey!" Isaac exclaimed. "Your arm!"

Hugh exhaled. He was hoping to deal with that issue later- once the ship had left the small moon and was safely in the expanse of space. "Yes. It's all better."

"I don't see how." Isaac looked at the arm again then looked at Gideon. "Are you sure it was as bad as you thought?"

"It was." Gideon put down his fork. "Does all the food taste like this?"

"Some of it is worse." Isaac lamented.

"We will discuss my arm and other things later. Once we are on our way."

"To Mars?" Hinata asked.

"Yes." Hugh flipped down a small black panel; there was a keyboard and a display behind it. "There we go." Since the displays seemed to all be touch-screens, he pressed the 'menu' icon then navigated to 'ship information' where he proceeded to change the ship's name. He left the ship's registry the same; Deimos but then also changed the ownership to 'Hugh Nunis' so there was still some connection to the previous owners but not a direct one, in case he was questioned. "Done."

"This makes food?" Hinata asked. He was looking at the food dispenser terminal. "I do not know what these words mean. Which one is rice? I have not had rice in almost four years."

"Isaac, explain the food to him. I need to get us going." Hugh said.

"Okay." Isaac answered. "There is no rice and the chili is disgusting but if you mix it with the macaroni it is much better. The steak is tough…" He began to explain the food options as Hugh headed toward the cockpit.

Twenty-Four

"Cynthia, confirm our transponder is showing *Knik Anchorage*." Hugh asked.

"Confirmed." Cynthia replied. "The ship is now designated *Knik Anchorage*."

"When are we out of eclipse?"

"Seven minutes." Cynthia replied.

"Perfect." Hugh tapped several icons bringing the engines online. "Okay, nice and easy." He slid the icon to increase the engine output as he pulled back on a lever. The ship rocked back and forth, banging the rear landing gear twice before finally taking off. "And that's why we landed way out here." He increased the engine output then gently moved the stick forward and to the right. The ship's nose dipped slightly then leveled out as it began to gain speed. Hugh let out a long sigh. "Here we go."

"Can I come in?" Gideon said after the door slid open.

"Sure, Gideon." Hugh said. "Have a seat here beside me." He gestured at the seat then quickly put his hand back on the attitude lever.

"You understand how to fly this?" Gideon asked as he sat.

"It's very much like a helicopter." He tapped the attitude lever. "This is like a cyclic and this." He looked at Gideon as his voice trailed off. "This… never mind." He smirked. "What's on your mind Gideon?"

"I have two questions; First, who are you and second, why are we going to Mars instead of back to Anchorage?" Gideon asked.

"The first part is complicated." Hugh began. "I'm not Amish, like I said before. I was just passing by the town and ended up staying there."

"And your arm?"

Hugh exhaled. "Okay, this is probably going to come out because Abigail already knows about me."

"That is my third question," Gideon interrupted. "How is it you are so familiar with my wife?"

"Whoa, settle down there." Hugh said. He piloted the ship past an outcropping as they skirted the surface of the moon. "It's nothing inappropriate." Hugh then thought back to when Abigail had seen him running naked in the woods. "Oh boy." He said.

"What?"

"What?" Hugh said. He glanced at Gideon. "No, it's nothing." He gestured at the viewscreen. "It may look like I am really good at this but honestly I am not. I only learned to fly this thing in the past week. And I had never been in space, much less another planet before this."

"Oh dear." Gideon said as he too looked at the viewscreens. "And you want to go to Mars? How far away is that? Can you even find it?"

"We'll be fine." Hugh said. "In any case," Hugh picked up where he had left off. "I have a disease that you are not familiar with. It's called vampirism."

"Vampirism?"

"Yes. And it had side effects that…" Hugh considered that. "Do you know what side effects are?" He had not spent any time with the town doctor so he wasn't sure what level of medicine the town was capable of.

"I understand side effects. Drinking too much apple cider causes the runs, for example." Gideon said testily. "Do you take me for a fool?"

"No, not at all. It's just… I come from a world that is far more advanced than your life in Anchorage and I sometimes don't know if the terms I am using are understood. And then I wonder if you Amish people just nod and agree without understanding because you don't want to be insulting or pester me with a lot of questions."

"I do not think that would be the case." Gideon said as he shook his head. "So Mars."

"What?"

"You come from Mars?"

"No; Earth." Hugh said. "More precisely Earth from over eighteen thousand years ago. I was frozen in a glacier in the year twenty twenty-six. The glacier thawed out in the year twenty-thousand twenty-seven. Eighteen thousand and one years. When I was frozen," Hugh pressed on, "I was six hundred sixty-seven years old at the time. So now." He looked at Gideon. "I am eighteen-thousand six-hundred sixty-eight years old."

"Listen Hugh." Gideon began. "I appreciate you rescuing me from that place. But there is no need to be rude; if you do not want to tell me, just say so. Lying to me is uncalled for."

Hugh held up his once-frozen hand and waggled his fingers. "Your own eyes saw my hand frozen. Now it's not. One of the other side-effects of vampirism is that I heal very quickly when I drink blood."

"Drink… blood?"

"Yes; I have to drink blood to stay alive." As soon as Hugh said it, he regretted it.

"Where do you get this blood that you need to drink?" Gideon started to get up out of the chair. "I'm…"

"Listen, Gideon." Hugh began. "You just have to trust me on this. You are not in any danger from me." He jerked a thumb backwards then returned his hands to the controls. "And neither are they." He arced around another outcropping. He was keeping the moon between them and the tracking station on Mars so that when they reappeared after a few minutes, if the same technician was watching they wouldn't suspect that the *Giselle* had suddenly -and illegally- become the *Knik Anchorage*. "Abigail trusts me and you should too."

"Yes, about *my wife*." Gideon said. "Why is it that you are so familiar with her?"

Hugh considered that for a moment. "To be honest with you, Gideon; Abigail saved me." He smirked. "She's a very headstrong woman. Amish upbringing notwithstanding. She's made me a better person." He smiled wide. "Slapped some sense into me is more accurate. Literally."

"Abigail has… has slapped you?" Gideon's eyes got big.

Hugh laughed. "Oh, I should warn you Brother Gideon, if you get her riled up you will be on the receiving end of a slap or a punch as well. She's something else." He got serious. "But listen to me Gideon; there is not a thing inappropriate between me and Abigail. She's the sister I wish I had."

"You don't have family?"

"I have no idea." Hugh shook his head. "I don't remember anything from before I contracted my disease. No family, no background, nothing. What is odd was that I could still read, write, build canoes, furniture, skin an animal. Everyday things I remembered; people I didn't. And with all the time that has passed, I am sure there are none around now."

"Oh. I see." Gideon said. He looked at the viewscreens again. "I admit I do not understand vampirism. How did you contract it? Is it contagious?"

Hugh frowned. The conversation was definitely not moving in the direction he wanted. "You don't need to be concerned. But one thing that is important is that Isaac does not know."

"Isaac does not know?"

"No way. If he knew, the entire town would know within a week." Hugh glanced at him. "I don't know how well you remember Isaac but he's…" Hugh smiled. "He's…"

"Yes. I remember Isaac." Gideon smirked as well. "He is a very talkative young man."

"Talkative. That is a good word for him." Hugh thought about what Hinata has said; *'insistent and chatty'*. He held up a finger. "But he is a good man who will do anything for you, so don't think I don't hold him in high regard." He opened his hand and panned around the ship. "He didn't blink twice at coming along in this ship if it meant getting you home to Abigail. They are very close as well, those two."

"They are very much like brother and sister." Gideon explained. "His mother died while he was young and his father was overwhelmed trying to raise five children on his own so Abigail stepped in and took Isaac under her wing."

"She's a trooper."

"What?" Gideon looked at him. "What is that?"

"Oh." Hugh considered the term. "She is willing to work extra to help others even at the sake of her own comfort and often puts the needs of others ahead of her own."

"She is definitely that; a trooper." Gideon said. "Hugh, you said you were new to flying this craft and I do not mean to insult you, but won't we have to get higher off the ground to get to Mars?"

"Oh man; that's rough." Hugh laughed. "Yes, we will indeed. I am just staying close to the surface because…" He stopped to decide how to explain it. "The authorities on Mars keep track of spacecrafts as they move around the planet and its two moons. They manage their paths so they don't run into each other. We are in a spacecraft that does not belong to us so I have changed its name and am flying close to Deimos until we are farther away from where they last saw us. Then we will make a big circle toward Mars, hopefully without them noticing it is the same ship. Hopefully."

"I don't understand how they can see us but." Gideon gestured at the controls. "I don't understand any of this."

"If you put your finger on the glass you can change where you are looking." Hugh reached over and moved the viewscreen around. "If you tap it twice with your finger it goes back to looking straight ahead. Oh, and when people talk to me you need to just keep quiet. Okay?"

"This ship doesn't belong to us?" Gideon asked. "This is stolen?"

"Wow, you two are a great pair; that's what Abigail would have gotten out of everything I said also." Hugh sighed. "It is more abandoned than anything else because the owners do not need it and are not looking for it anymore."

"I am not sure that is the entire truth."

"It's pretty damned close." Hugh said. "Okay." He pointed at the middle viewscreen. "We're heading up. If you see anything appear on that window there, let me know; I'm going to be concentrating on the ones in front of me." Hugh banked the ship one last time then arced gracefully upward and away from Deimos. Within moments, Mars filled the viewscreen in front of him. As he turned, it moved over to the side of the viewscreen and disappeared.

"You are missing Mars."

"I'm going to go around it in a big circle because I am not sure where we need to land yet. And I want to land during the day when people are at work."

"Who is it we are seeing on Mars?"

"The leader of the planet and its two moons. He's called a governor."

"I know the term." Gideon replied.

"Oh. I'm sorry; I figured since you didn't have one…" His voice trailed off. "We're going to see the governor of Mars because I'm going to demand that he… or she, stop the practice of what you call A Gathering."

"Do you think he or she will listen? The humans I saw seemed very amused by us being in cages and Hinata told me it was the same in the other place he was as well. If it brings them amusement why would they stop? They do not seem to put much thought into the feelings of each other, much less prisoners like us."

"Because I can be very persuasive." Hugh said. For a moment he considered changing in front of Gideon, then decided against it. The man had already been given a lot of information to digest in a very short amount of time. "Even if they don't want to, they will have to listen to what I have to say because I will be right in front of them. Maybe I can plant the seed that what they are doing is wrong." He gave a smile. "Hopefully that will work." He added, when in reality the plan he had in his mind was much more up close and personal. And far more threatening. Which is why he was planning on leaving Gideon in the

Knik Anchorage when he delivered his ultimatum. He was considering bringing Hinata- if he could control his homicidal tendencies.

"So we are going straight there then?" Gideon asked.

"No, not exactly. I am going to take a couple of days to practice docking." He gestured at the controls. "I'm still new at this and I don't want to run into anything."

"I understand." Gideon said. Even though he didn't know what docking was. It sounded important however and he did not want to pester Hugh with more questions. "Yes; that makes sense."

Twenty-Five

"I hope you appreciate that I sent for you, Brother Iddo." Eli said. He was sitting with Freeman and Jacob who were also on the council. "I did not want to speak out of turn."

"I do appreciate it." Iddo said. "Even though I feel that this is a waste of time, because the fact of the matter is..."

"Brother Iddo," Freeman interrupted. "We agreed that Eli would be allowed to speak first."

"The issue at hand," Iddo said ignoring Freeman, "is that we have a murderous animal in our midst. And that some of the people of this town seem to be just fine with that fact."

"Now see here!" Eli said loudly. "Brother Iddo, you are speaking out of turn and I am not going to allow it." Took several calming breaths than put his hands on the table. "There is indeed someone in our town who comes from a different time and he used to lead a very different life. A very different life than he does now, I should add." Eli looked at Iddo. "I agree that he used to lead a hostile life. But he has changed for the better." He raised a hand, "But that is not why this meeting has been called. It has been called because I believe that Brother Iddo's judgement has been clouded by his feelings toward Hugh. And because of that, I don't see him willing to listen to any sort of reason."

"I shall listen." Iddo gestured with his hand. "Speak, Brother Eli. And I shall listen."

"What is it that you have against Hugh?" Eli asked.

Iddo looked at the three men at the table, then at Eli directly. "What Brother Eli does not know is that I have personally seen this Hugh hunting. Hunting bear and moose."

"Brother Iddo," Freeman said. "Bear and moose are hunted often. I do not see how that could be an issue."

Eli exhaled slowly. Abigail had explained to him what Hugh was doing for sustenance; it seemed like a very good compromise. "Brother Iddo."

"I am not concerned with *what* he hunts; it is the *way* he does it."

"Brother Iddo." Eli tried again.

"*No* Brother Eli, you have brought the subject up and I will bring it to light." He leaned forward in his chair. "When he hunts, he is *naked!*"

Eli let out a laugh. "Oh." He tried stifling it. "Sorry, sorry. It's just that…" He laughed again.

"It is no laughing matter!" Iddo said. "It is disgraceful and sinful. What if he is seen by one of the women of the town?"

"Brother Iddo, please." Eli was still chuckling. "Oh, I am sorry; you have caught me completely unawares."

"Unawares?" Iddo said with a frown.

"Yes. You see, I was worried you were going to discuss…" Eli stopped. He wasn't prepared to discuss Hugh's eating habits. "I apologize. I understand how Hugh hunting without clothes is definitely inappropriate. However Sister Abigail has seen to it that…"

"Sister Abigail has seen Hugh hunting naked?" Iddo leaned back in his seat. "Oh dear!"

"Brother Iddo, please." Eli put his hand on the man's arm. "Rest easy. Sister Abigail has made Hugh hunting clothes. He is now covered properly when he hunts."

"Brother Eli," Freeman said. "I am sorry, I do not understand; Hugh hunted naked and now he has hunting clothes? I do not understand what is being discussed here. Although I agree that he should not run around naked. That is very improper."

"Yes, of course." Eli said. "Well the issue was…the reason how Hugh hunts is…" Eli hesitated. "Oh dear."

"Is what?" Jacob asked.

"Hugh has a condition." Eli began. "An illness, really." He put his hands back on the table. "Brothers, please remain calm as I explain and let me finish my explanation entirely."

"Proceed." Freeman said.

"Hugh has a condition called vampirism. It requires that he drink blood to remain alive."

"What? How can this be; I have eaten dinner with him." Jacob said. "He ate what we ate."

Eli nodded. "I have eaten many times with him as well. He can eat and drink like we do, but that does not sustain him. So he hunts."

"He drinks the blood of moose and bear?" Jacob asked. "I do not understand that, but if that is what he needs…" Now he hesitated. "Why… is he naked?"

"Because he hunts them barehanded." Eli said.

"Moose?" Jacob's eyes got large. "And bear?"

"He has extraordinary abilities. He is quite strong, and heals quickly. He can even see in the dark."

"Like that Benfleet. His affliction?" Freeman asked. "Oh my."

Eli shook his head. "Only partially. Benfleet also had the Madness. He could not be reasoned with because of it."

"Benfleet ate people." Freeman said. "So does Hugh also…" His voice trailed off.

Eli was dreading that particular part of Hugh's past but knew that to be able to have Hugh accepted, he couldn't hide the things he had done. "Yes. *But in the past.*" Eli added quickly. "Hugh has not killed anyone since he came into our village that night several months ago."

Brother Iddo raised his eyebrows and cleared his throat.

"Yes, Brother Iddo; I am aware that Hugh most likely killed those four gatherers that came to our town. It was apparently unavoidable. The situation spiraled out of his control."

"He also killed Benfleet." Iddo pointed out.

"That was self-defense. Benfleet was trying to kill Hugh to eat him in hopes it could cure his malady. Since they were both afflicted with vampirism, Benfleet hoped Hugh could heal his madness." Eli explained. He smiled again. "And as it was pointed out to me by two young carpenters, we all have done things in our past that we no longer do now."

Iddo shook his head. "We shall not stoop to talking about the elimination of waste."

"What?" Jacob said.

Eli waved a hand dismissively. "Youthful banter. But pertinent; Amos pointed out that in his youth, he used to fill his diapers. But now he is better."

"My word." Jacob said, shocked.

"While crass, the young man has a point. He has learned to not do such things. Just as Hugh is learning that killing people is wrong." Eli said.

"How could anyone not know that?" Freeman asked.

"Hugh is not a believer, Brother Freeman." Eli explained. "While he may be able to quote scripture," he gestured at Iddo, "as I pointed out to Brother Iddo, he may be able to quote it but doesn't take it to heart."

"Well if he knows it, then that is halfway there, I would think." Brother Jacob said.

"That is what I said as well." Eli said. He gestured at Iddo again. "When I spoke to Brother Iddo, I said that too. But, Brothers that is not why I asked to speak to you here and now."

"I was under the assumption this discussion was whether Hugh could remain in town." Iddo said. "It is not?"

"Well, in a way it is." Eli said. "But from another discussion with those two youngsters, something else came up." He raised a finger. "A solution to an ongoing problem we have. A good solution to it if it is successful, I might add."

"What problem is that?" Jacob asked.

"Violent incursions from the Inuit."

"So now we are back to Hugh being our attack dog against the Inuit?"

"Of course not, Brother Iddo," Eli said. "What I would like to propose is that with the assistance and protection of Hugh, I go to the main Inuit city, Fair Banks and propose to the Inuit Grand Governor an accord between our two people."

"An accord?" Freeman scoffed. "The Inuit are violent people that will not listen to anything you have to say."

"Hugh can be very persuasive." Eli said. "If he can hunt a moose barehanded, I am sure he can get the Inuit to listen to me." He raised a finger. "Oh, and he also speaks Inuit. They will *have* to listen to him."

"That would indeed be helpful since you do not speak Inuit." Jacob said.

"Hugh speaks it as well as several other languages. He has lived a very long time and has learned multiple languages in that time." Eli said. "So, Hugh can help translate for me."

"To what end?" Iddo asked curiously.

"A peaceful accord. Inuit will be free to travel and visit our towns and the other Amish communities. They can trade and such and we will do the same with them. There would be no more violence." Eli said.

"I do not see how you would be able to make such an agreement; these are violent people." Jacob said. When Eli began to speak, he raised a hand. "*However*, if there is a chance that it could work, then I believe we should try it. For the betterment of all Amish people, ending this violence should be our ultimate endeavor." Now Jacob smiled. "And if the Inuit do come into our towns peacefully, then perhaps we can witness to them as well."

"Exactly," Eli said. "If first with the Inuit, then perhaps with the Wildmen to the south. After all, we are charged with spreading the Good News instead of just keeping it within our city limits, are we not?"

"That is true." Jacob replied. "Still it is fraught with danger, this plan of yours."

Brother Iddo nodded. "I agree it is dangerous for Brother Eli so I am hesitant. The risks are great. While we do disagree on the topic of Hugh, we usually stand together. I worry greatly that you wouldn't return from your visit to the Inuit city." Iddo shook his head. "And I do not see how just having Hugh with you would make such an endeavor successful. Two surrounded in an entire city of enemies?"

Eli did not want to mention the change that Hugh went through when he became a vampire for fear the council would forbit the plan. "He is very persuasive." He said simply.

"Yes, but are you?" Iddo asked.

"What?"

"Will you be able to convince them that we should all live in peace?"

"No one has ever even tried it." Eli pointed out. "I think the surprise of us walking into their town alone would make them want to hear what we have to say."

"Will Hugh even be willing to go on such an expedition? Why should he be willing to put himself in danger for us?" Iddo asked.

Eli had hoped that Iddo would ask that question. He beamed. "I am glad you asked. Because Brother Iddo, this is now his home as well. And he cares for the people in it."

Iddo smirked as he pointed a finger at Eli. "How long have you been waiting for me to ask that question, you old fox?"

"Truth be told, since right before I went to sleep last night." Eli replied.

"You are a rascal, Eli." Iddo said with a headshake. "Those poor Inuit won't know what to think of the word games you will confuse them with." He waved a hand. "Fine then. Go old friend. And I shall pray for your safe return to tell the tale."

"For both our returns, I'd hope." Eli winked at the man.

"Yes, yes. For both you and Hugh to return safe and sound. Of course." Iddo added.

"Then it is settled." Jacob looked at the ceiling. "When he returns, you can speak to him about this. And if he is willing, you both go with our blessings."

Eli nodded. Hoping that Hugh would be willing to make such a trip. He decided he would have Abigail present when he presented his plan to have a better chance of success.

Twenty-Six

"This is *Knik Anchorage* requesting a slot at Gate Five. Any color is fine." Hugh said nonchalantly. He had questioned Cynthia at length about the location of political offices on Mars as well as landing procedures and terminology. While there were literally thousands of landing stations around the city, the closest landing station to Governor Sykes' office used by non-resident ships was Gate Five. It would put him about a mile from the office, in fact. Which considering the size of the city- which it truly was instead of just a town, was better than he had hoped for.

As Hugh had flown over the domed city of Burke (named after one of its founders), he was amazed at its size; it was seventy-five miles long and thirty miles wide; bigger than Los Angeles in the 21st Century by almost a hundred square miles. There were huge swaths of green forests and fields and according to Cynthia three hundred thousand people lived under the thousand-foot high, flexible dome. The dome was held in place above the city using hundreds of weighted anchors on the end of cables that just hung in space in a geosynchronous orbit, much like the 'space elevator' technology that had been used for centuries on several of Jupiter's larger moons and for the floating cities on Venus. Burke was the largest city in the Solar System, with Sulci Gordi at the base of Olympus Mons coming in second with two hundred thousand citizens. A dozen other smaller towns were scattered around the planet from pole to pole. All in all, almost a fifth of the entire population of the Solar System lived on Mars. It was the de facto capital for space faring Humans.

"Roger, *Knik Anchorage*," a voice responded. "What is your destination and purpose?"

Hugh was prepared for the question: "Dropping off some art to a private collector."

"Living or stuffed?"

"Living." Hugh looked at Hinata who was sitting in the copilot seat and smiled. "So far."

Hinata bared his teeth at him.

"Be advised you are responsible for the safety of the citizens of Burke. Any issues will result in fines equaling twice the manpower costs required to deal with said issues."

"Just like last time. Got it." Hugh held his finger to his lip to make sure Hinata didn't say anything. "Where am I plugging in?"

"Continue on current course. You will be in slot blue seventeen, Gate Six." The voice replied. "Transfer control to Gate Six Ops for docking."

"Oh." Hugh was taken aback. "I was hoping for Gate Five; less walking, you know?"

"Lazy?" The voice sounded amused.

"Closer to my drop off, Ops." Hugh said. "Less time wandering around putting the safety of the citizens of Burke in danger." He hesitated. "As well as my profit margin. This is brand new art."

"If your cargo is dangerous, you need to make the proper arrangements."

Hugh looked at Hinata again. "Negative, Ops. Cargo is properly subdued and compliant."

Hinata made a fist.

"But cutting down variables keeps plans from going sideways." Hugh continued. "But if six is all you have…" His voice trailed off.

"We can put you at Gate Five, red, slot twelve." Mars Operations said. "Passing your telemetry to Gate Five. Prepare to relinquish controls."

"Ready and waiting." Hugh hovered his finger above the appropriate icon to allow the operations center to pilot the ship in. Once Cynthia had explained that all docking at major cities was automated to ensure there were no mishaps, Hugh decided to go straight to the city instead of wasting time practicing docking procedures. Waiting only until it was ten in the morning in Burke, which took the better part of a day, ship's time.

"*Knik Anchorage*, this is Gate Five, over?" A new voice said.

"Hear you, Gate Five. Ready and waiting."

"Initiate."

Hugh nodded as he tapped the icon. Immediately the ship veered off to the side, diving toward the massive city. He let out a sigh of relief. "Better you than me." He looked at Hinata. "I'm still not sure I want to bring you along."

"I will be of assistance in the event something goes wrong."

"Nothing should go wrong."

"Hah!" Hinata laughed. "If only that were the case, I would be still living on my farm with my family. Yes, nothing should ever go wrong, but it often does."

Hugh frowned. "Just remember I am not going down there to try and kill every single person. I'm there to talk to the Governor. Just talk."

"I understand Hugh-san." Hinata watched the viewscreens as the ship sailed downward. "I will do what you ask and I will be your eyes behind your back."

"Well, that would be helpful yes."

Twenty-Seven

"Hinata, just relax." Hugh whispered. They were standing on a fairly busy street waiting for someone to enter the large government complex they were in front of so they could sneak in behind them. Hugh had Officer Hazelgrove's glove still but was worried it was now programmed to set off alarms if he tried to use it. He was saving it for a dire emergency.

"I am on a leash like a *dog*." Hinata seethed. "The embarrassment is more than anyone can bear."

"How can you be embarrassed?" Hugh gestured across the area. "It's not like you know any of these people. And you'll never see them again anyway. We are undercover deep in the enemy's territory. The last thing we need is a bunch of people noticing us."

"Huh!" He said. He crossed his arms and looked at his feet. "They should all should taste my blade!"

A passerby gave them a sidelong look.

Hugh smiled at the man and jerked a thumb at Hinata. "He's new."

The Martian shook his head and continued on his way.

Hinata looked up at the sky; the street was bright thanks to the lights from the buildings but the sky itself was dark and even under the covered dome, there was an orange haze in the sky. "Even in the morning it is dark?"

"The sun is farther away than on Earth." Hugh explained. "Which I appreciate."

"And there is just a covering over the city? That is all between it and the space where there is no air?"

"Yes, but it's more than a covering like a blanket or something. It's eight feet thick and auto-repairing, Cynthia said." Hugh explained.

"I wonder what it would take to cut a great hole in it." Hinata put his hand on his wakizashi; the smaller of his two blades. He refused to leave the ship with no weapon so Hugh had to make a concession. It was tucked into his loose-fitting pants with just the tip of the hilt showing. Hugh hoped it was not sticking out enough for a quick, poorly thought-out attack.

"Stop it." Hugh said. "You're going to get us unwanted attention." He turned to face him. "And while you are formidable with that little weapon, and I am as well, the pair of us are no match for an entire city's law enforcement. We will both end up in cages for the rest of our lives." He poked Hinata in the chest. "And in case you forgot, for me that's probably *forever*. So quiet down."

"Is there a problem here?"

Hugh turned to look. It was a tall thin police officer. "What's that officer?" He fell into his 'ask questions' routine.

"Is there a problem here?" The officer asked again. He pointed at Hinata. "With that?"

Hugh gestured at Hinata. "Him? No. Not at all. Just doing a delivery is all Officer." He smiled. "Then I'll be on my way." He shook his head. "He's my last delivery of the day. I'm beat."

"Then why are you loitering here on the street?"

"I was just taking in the sights, Officer." Hugh put a hand on his hip in what he hoped was a friendly gesture. "Taking in the sights. This is nothing like Venus, I can tell you that. Have you ever been to Venus?"

"No." The Officer said. He eyed Hinata up and down.

"Blue skies, breezes. You should visit." Hugh patted him on the shoulder. "Get out and see the sights. Live a little. Am I right?"

The officer looked down at his shoulder where Hugh had patted it. "You need to get on with…"

Behind them, a woman pressed her hand on the entry pad. When the large double doors opened, she stepped in.

"Oh, crud. There goes Cynthia." Hugh pointed at the woman. "Oh man! I'm going to lose my tip. Sorry Officer, got to go." He moved quickly to the door, yanking Hinata with him. To add to the lie he called, "Miss Cynthia!"

Since the woman's name wasn't Cynthia, she just kept walking.

Hugh continued, pulling a foot-shuffling Hinata with him. He didn't look back until the doors closed behind him. The officer had remained outside. He stopped and put his hands on his knees. "Oh man. That was close."

"I could have cut him down where he stood." Hinata said.

"Yeah, great idea Hinata." Hugh said. "Great idea. The pair of us standing there with a murdered police officer. I'm sure that would go great for us, right?" He scowled. "I knew bringing you was a mistake." He tapped his head. "All you have is a mind for revenge."

"It is all I seek."

"Well I seek getting back to Earth and bringing Gideon to his wife who is expecting us. That's what I seek. If you want to get yourself killed, that's fine by me. When we get back to the ship, you can just wander off and kill as many people as you can before you are gunned down."

"What is a gunned?"

"It's gun. It is a weapon that can be used to kill you without even being close to you." Hugh explained. "You wouldn't even have a chance against the person using it because it sends small pieces of metal hundreds of feet. And when they stick in you, they kill you."

"It is like a bow then."

"Only smaller and far more deadly." Hugh said. He yanked on the leash. "So let's go. I will say what I want to say to the governor then you are free to do what you want. Right?"

"Fine." Hinata nodded. "That is acceptable."

Hugh looked around. "Office twenty-five twelve. That means probably the twenty-fifth floor. We need to find the elevators."

"The what?"

"Just keep quiet. You're supposed to be a meek prisoner, remember? So keep quiet."

"Hai." Hinata looked down at his feet. "Hai, Hugh-san. Let us find this *ele-vator*."

Hugh moved to the middle of the large foyer where they were eight elevators arranged four per side. There were a few people here and there, however no security. Between each of the pairs was a listing of offices. After only a moment, Hugh found the Governor's office; it was indeed on the twenty fifth floor. He pressed the button to call the elevator then took a couple of steps back from the large double doors. "Move back here Hinata." He said. "So folks can get out."

"Get out of what? Is that a room?"

Hugh shook his head. "No. It is a box that is on a cable that carries people up and down to the different floors of the building. Otherwise we would have to walk twenty-five flights up." He pointed upwards. "And that is a long way."

"Hai." Hinata said. "My friend had a home with three stories. The children were on the topmost floor even though the breezes there were better because Arata did not want to walk up there every day." He smiled.

"Well, when we get home, I can take you there and you can visit with your friend Arata." Hugh said. "That's better than trying to hack your way through this city, right?"

"Arata is dead. So is everyone else in my village." Hinata spread his arms out wide. "These people killed them all."

"You were the only one that wasn't killed out of your entire village?" Hugh looked at him. "How did that happen?"

"These visitors came..."

As the doors of the elevator opened, Hugh held a finger to his lips. The pair stood there quietly as several people got out. When it was empty, he gestured. "Get in."

Hinata cautiously stepped into the elevator. "Devil box." He said.

"Probably." Hugh stepped in behind him. When two men tried to get in, he gestured at Hinata. "Take the next one, he's been in a mood all day."

The two Martians nodded knowingly.

"You better put it in its place." One said. "Nip that attitude in the bud."

"That's why I have kid art. They're easier to keep quiet." The other said. "Then dump them at ten."

"Once they're in double digits, they're good for other things." The first leered. "Know what I mean?"

"Oh boy." Hugh glanced at Hinata. "Thanks for the advice." He pressed the 'close doors' button repeatedly. When the doors finally closed, he looked at Hinata. "Good job not saying anything."

"Children? Children! You see now why they need to die, Hugh-san. All of them. Talk is not what they need. They need *death*. And I can give it to them."

Hugh pressed the button for the twenty-fifth floor. "Let's just try to get out of the building without anyone noticing us."

Twenty-Eight

Hugh looked at the numbers as they scrolled by on the screen. "Well, let's try talking first. So these visitors came to your village?" He coaxed.

"Yes; visitors came to my village. We had never seen them before so we welcomed them." He gave a curt nod. "Proper hosts do such things." He scowled. "Then they showed their treachery at a feast that night when they declared they were taking four of us with them."

"It's always four. Very strange." Hugh commented.

"It was me, and three others. Three women. Risa, Mizuko, and Wakako. So we fought them. We men. We fought like tigers." Hinata shook his head. "And they subdued the four of us then destroyed the entire village with lightning from their ship. They made us watch as they did it."

"Where are the three women?" Hugh asked. Wondering if getting them back could put Hinata on a different -less murderous- path.

"They all killed themselves before we got to Mars." Hinata sighed. "They told them what they would be used for when they got to Mars. They were being sent to the mines."

"They were going to make them miners?" Hugh shook his head. "I don't see how…"

"They would be used *by* the miners as entertainment." Hinata cut him off. "The shame was too much for them to bear." He put his hand on the hilt of his sword. "They used this to kill themselves. Now I will use it to avenge their deaths and wash their blood off it."

"Oh man. Hinata, that's…" The elevator doors opened. "Let's go." Hugh said as he stepped into the corridor at the front of a very large foyer.

"And before you ask, I vowed to make these people pay." Hinata said as he stepped beside him. "Just as you have given your word, so have I." There was a large empty pedestal in the center of the foyer and three doors spaced evenly around the broad curve behind it. "We are men of our word, are we not, Hugh-san?"

"We are indeed, Hinata-kun." Hugh said, using the male honorific instead of the more generic 'san'. He pointed. "Twelve, there on the right. Takes up that whole side of the building, it looks like."

"Let us be done with this then." Hinata started toward the door.

"You should wait out here." Hugh said.

"Wait out here?"

"If I need you I'll give a shout."

Hinata narrowed his eyes. "Wait out here… doing what?"

"Nothing." Hugh said. "Don't kill anyone. Don't talk to anyone." He pointed. "Go stand on that pedestal over there."

Hinata looked. "What? Stand there like some trained monkey?"

"If anyone asks, tell them you are the Governor's new traveling art." Hugh shrugged. "If anyone asks that is. I doubt anyone would even talk to you."

"Huh." Hinata stalked to the platform and stepped onto it. "The embarrassment is overwhelming. Go talk, Hugh. So we may leave this place." He put his hands on his hips and scowled.

Hugh nodded. "Right." He walked to the door. There was no handle on the outside. "Huh."

Hinata laughed. "Hah! The mighty Hugh-san stopped by an uncooperative door."

Hugh looked around. Waiting in the large foyer for someone to show up was not a good idea. "Okay, I'm going to try something."

"Like you did back on the moon?" Hinata's eyes got large.

"Yes. So just keep quiet."

"Hai." Hinata said. He turned so he could watch. When Hugh started to say something, he raised a hand. "I will watch quietly."

Hugh closed his eyes and took several breaths. He concentrated on nothingness.

After several moments Hinata whispered. "Nothing is happening Hugh-san. I thought I should let you know."

"Just give me a minute." Hugh snapped. He relaxed more and thought of nothingness. Nothingness in his arms. Nothingness in his legs. His entire body.

"Ahhh," Hinata whispered very softly.

Hugh ignored him and continued to clear his mind.

"Devil magic." Hinata whispered again.

Hugh continued to concentrate on nothingness. Unsure if anything was happening, he tried to open his eyes and realized he was aware of everything in the area. He could see the room around him in all directions. For a moment, he began to panic, then realized that what had happened. He turned his attention -since he really didn't have eyes- toward the door.

It looked like the same regular solid door but now he was aware that the edges of it along the side, top, and bottom were open. It seemed to him the gaps were a mile across. He began to move toward the bottom crack and into the room past it, easily passing through the wide spaces.

As he went, he became aware of not only the foyer, but the room beyond the door. He couldn't see what was beyond the large desk in front of him; it obscured the rest of the room, but to the left was a long conference table with high-back leather chairs. On the right was a seating area with overstuffed seats. He moved along the floor, staying low as he headed toward the seating area. He became aware that there was someone else in the room; he could hear someone speaking even though he did not have ears that he was aware of.

Unfathomable he thought. Absently he wondered if he would have clothes when he re-appeared. Coalesced? He wasn't even sure what word to use to describe what was happening. He reached the seating area and saw that the man who was speaking was standing and facing away from him, looking out large windows onto the city below. A red haze clouded the far-off view.

Hugh began to think about his body. His arms. And legs. Thinking how they had substance. How he looked day to day. He flexed his hands; they now seemed solid to him so he looked down. He was in indeed whole again, and in the room. But naked. He fought to keep a chuckle from escaping. He was sure that both times when Benfleet began to turn into a mist then reappeared, his clothes did so with him. *Practice is what you need, Hugh*. He thought. *How are you going to be imposing when you're stark naked?* He gave a shrug and padded quietly toward the man- Governor Sykes.

Twenty-Nine

"I don't really care what they are upset about, Gregory." Sykes snapped. "They either get back to work or they can find someplace else to live besides Burke and you can lead the way!" The man nodded several times. "Yeah. Fine, *fine*. I don't really care as long as the magnesium mines stay open." He looked up at the ceiling. "End transmission!" He snapped. He put his hands on his hips while looking out at the cityscape. "Idiot."

Hugh was practically on top of Sykes and the man did not seem to be aware. Hugh smirked. "Believe me, this isn't how I planned this meeting to go." He said.

Sykes jumped at the sound of Hugh's voice and turned quickly. He looked from Hugh's face to the locked door, then back to Hugh. "How did you get in here?" His eyes moved down. "Oh, wait a minute. Just wait a minute!"

"Calm down, Governor," Hugh scowled. "I'm really going to have to work on that." He turned his head toward the door. "Unlock that door."

"No way. You're… you're crazy! How did you even get in here?"

Hugh turned his head back around as he changed. "Unlock that door now!" He growled in the man's face. He bared his fangs. "Or we're done talking."

"What?" Sykes stumbled backwards against the windows. "What is going on?"

"Open that door or I'm going to see if this gravity will kill you at twenty-five stories." Hugh took a step toward him. "Open it now!"

"I'll have you shot!" Sykes said as he stepped close to Hugh. He was a full head taller than Hugh. "I'll have you pitched into the deepest mine I own!"

Hugh grabbed handfuls of the man's shirt under his armpits, picking him up. He took two steps forward and banged him against the windows. "I wonder which is stronger; these windows or your backbone."

"Put me down!"

Hugh banged the man hard against the window again. This time cracks developed in it. "Oh, looks like we'll have to see how well your attitude works against gravity." He pulled the man back and slammed him into the glass again. The cracks spread out from behind the man. "Well?"

The man stared at Hugh.

Hugh took five large steps back and charged the glass again. This time several pieces fell out, the wind outside at 25 stories whistled as it entered the room. "From the looks of that glass, one more time and you're flying. Or you open the door." Hugh pulled the man back and again took five steps back preparing to rush at the glass. "Personally, I can fly so I'm not too worried. My partner out there has a death wish, so he's okay if I just leave him to kill as many Martians as he can manage."

"Door, open." The man said. Dutifully the door clacked open.

"Hinata, get in here!" Hugh shouted.

"Who are you?" Sykes scowled. "You stinking shorter! Some do-gooder Venetian? Some rock-hopper? Damned genetic engineers."

"I'm from *Earth*." Hugh threw the man toward the seating area. Thanks to Mars' gravity, he was able to easily throw the man the thirty feet. He banged into the chairs sideways, slowing his fall then he rolled against the wall.

Hinata entered the room. "Hugh-san, your clothes!" He held up Hugh's clothes and shoes. He smiled wide. "I am not sure if that is an honorable method of travel."

Hugh moved quickly to Hinata. "Give me those." He pointed at the governor. "And make sure he doesn't move. He might call reinforcements."

"Hai!" Hinata drew his blade.

"Do not kill him." Hugh said. "I'm not done talking to him."

Hinata glanced at the broken window as he advanced on the governor. "I approve of your method of talking." He pointed the blade at him. "Do not move or you will taste my blade."

"You stupid primitives!" Sykes started to work himself to his feet. "I'll have you both…"

Hinata stabbed Sykes in the shoulder.

"Hey!" Hugh was hopping into his pants. "I said don't kill him."

"That is not a fatal strike." Hinata gestured with his sword. "I can do that *dozens* of times and still not put his life at risk." He glowered at the man. "NOW SIT DOWN!"

The man slid onto his butt. "What do think you are accomplishing?" He pressed his hand against his bleeding shoulder. Even though it wasn't deep, it still hurt. "You stupid primitives."

"SILENCE!" Hinata put the blade against the man's calf. "I will not ask again!"

The man's attention was focused on the bloody blade pressed hard against his calf. He realized that he could indeed be stuck dozens of times in his extremities and still survive, so he didn't say anything.

"Don't let him push any buttons or touch his watch." Hugh said-he was putting on his shirt.

"What is a watch?"

The governor stifled a chuckle.

"It is a device for keeping time," Hugh said. "It is on his wrist. It also lets him talk to others so he could call for help with it."

"I shall cut that hand off then." Hinata raised his blade high in the air. "Wakkata?" (Okay)

"Īe" Hugh replied (No)

Hinata smiled. "Hugh-san, you speak more Japanese than you let on. How long did you live in my homeland?"

"I've never been." Hugh sat to put on his boots. "But I spent a lot of time in San Francisco, in Chinatown. But there were a lot of Japanese there also."

"You mean New San Francisco." The governor said. "On Pallas."

Hugh chuckled. "That's always bugged me. Why can't people in the future just come up with new names for cities? I saw it in movies all the time; 'New London, New San Francisco, New New York'. Here's a news flash for you; they were crap holes to start with; the universe doesn't need a new crap hole Detroit."

"What are you talking about? What movies?" The governor asked; he decided since the man was addressing him it was okay to answer—even though the one standing over him now held his blade over his head ready to strike.

"Here's another shocker for you, Governor Sykes." Hugh stood and tugged his shirt down. "I'm from the year twenty twenty-six." He held up a finger as he approached. "Two thousand twenty-six; there's no hidden zero in there."

The governor shook his head. "You're insane."

Hugh rushed at the man, moving faster than any human could, changing as he did. When he got to him, he grabbed him and picked him up high. "No; I'm an immortal vampire!" He lowered the man as he opened his mouth wide- it opened wider than it should have been able to, his long fangs gleaming as saliva dripped down them.

"Kill him, Hugh-san. Bite his head off!" Hinata smiled wide. "But slowly so he knows what is happening."

"Wait! Wait!" Sykes pleaded. "Stop!"

Hugh laughed. "Oh yeah, you're a much better sidekick than Isaac."

"Kare o korosu." Hinata said (Kill him)

"Īe" Hugh leaned in closer.

"Stop!" The man continued to plead.

Hugh scowled at the governor. "You are going to sit and you are going to listen to what I have to say. If you do anything that annoys me, I will rip your throat out." He lowered the man to the floor but continued to crowd him. "You should know that is not a figure of speech." He changed back to human form. "I will *literally* grab your esophagus and pull it out of your neck and watch you drown on your own blood. And if you call for help, I will rip your throat out then disappear and your security will think you're crazy." He held up his hand and concentrated on it. His fingertips turned into whisps of smoke, then the palm of his hand faded from sight as well.

"What?" Sykes eyes got large. He swiveled them over to Hinata.

"Oh, he's just a regular human." Hugh said as his hand reappeared. "But he wants to kill as many Martians as he can before he dies."

"Oh, that is indeed my wish." Hinata brought his small sword to the ready. "I only wish I had my katana so I could kill more of you before I am gunned."

"What?" The governor said, honestly confused by the statement.

"We got off subject there for a moment." Hugh said. "You will sit, you will listen. If you do, I won't kill you." He gestured at Hinata. "And I won't let him do it either. You have my word."

Sykes chuckled. "Your word. The word of a…" His voice trailed off. "I mean…"

Hugh tossed Sykes into one of the chairs. "I need you alive so you will do what I tell you. Dead, I'd have to start all over again with your second; Deputy Governor Carlson." He grimaced. "And she looks like a screamer to me." Hugh jabbed a finger at him. "So listen carefully."

"Okay, okay. Uhm…" Sykes' voice trailed off.

"Hugh. I'm Hugh."

"Okay, Mister Hugh. I'm all ears." Sykes let out a long breath, trying to calm himself. Being on the receiving end of threats was a new experience for him. "What do you have to say?"

"Watch the door, Hinata." Hugh said.

"What?" Hinata looked from the pair of them to the door and back.

"I will speak loud enough for you to hear. Even if he doesn't call someone, there is the chance that someone will come to see the Governor of Mars for some official business while we're here."

"Ahh, right, right." Hinata moved to the door, sword at the ready.

"Your practice of capturing Humans and bringing them here as slaves, or art, or whatever else you do with them will stop." Hugh said flatly.

Sykes chuckled. "Oh, is that all? I thought you were going to ask for something big." He clapped his hands together once. "Done."

"It is that simple?" Hinata asked.

Hugh frowned. "He is making a joke of it. He has no intentions of stopping."

"Why should we? Those primitives don't have any rights. It's like having a dog as a pet. Or a monkey."

"Animals are treated better!" Hinata tightened his grip on his sword. "Just kill him Hugh."

Hugh slapped Sykes across the face, bloodying his lip. "The thing is, Sam; you don't have a choice."

"Oh I think I have lots of choices." He glanced at the door.

Hugh crossed his arms. "Mars is really nice. It's kind of Earth-like in some ways. In other ways, not at all." He gestured at the windows. "It's what; eleven in the morning right now? And I can walk around without any problem at all. Back on Earth?" He shook his head. "Very uncomfortable." He leaned down closer. "And the thing is Sam, popular literature seems to be pretty accurate when it comes to vampires." Hugh held up his hand. "We can turn to smoke, fly, control people's minds." He leaned in closer and allowed just his fangs to grow. "And we're *contagious.* Just imagine if on my way out of town, I bit a few Martians. Let's say just an even dozen. And without anyone giving them any sort of guidance, that dozen would easily infect a dozen each in their first week. Twelve times twelve is a hundred forty-four. A hundred forty-four immature, angry vampires running around your city. By the next week that number would be…" He looked at the ceiling. "What is a hundred forty-four times twelve? Go ahead and ask."

"Tiberius, what is a hundred forty-four times twelve?" Sykes asked.

"One thousand seven hundred twenty-eight." The AI answered immediately.

"Tiberius, what is one thousand seven hundred twenty-eight times twelve?" Hugh asked.

Sykes' eyes got large.

"Twenty thousand seven hundred thirty-six." Tiberius answered.

"And that's just the first month." Hugh smiled. "Imagine where your domed city will be in six months. Why, I imagine that the rest of the system, seeing what is happening would blockade the entire planet and then nuke Burke from space. Then because from what I've read, the Venusians don't really care for you Thinners," Hugh continued, using the disparaging term the shorter, stockier Venusians used for the tall, thin Martians, "they'd nuke the rest of the cities on the planet just in case."

"Now wait a minute." Sykes said. "You're talking about killing almost a million people!"

"I'm a vampire." Hugh shrugged. "I kill people for *lunch*."

"Hugh-san." Hinata said. "That sounds like a perfect plan. Let us do that."

"He's not even a vampire and he's on board." Hugh gestured at Hinata.

"What?" Sykes asked. "What did we do to you?"

"Oh, Governor, you have done more than you can imagine." Hinata said as he stalked toward him. "I do not know what this nuke thing is, but any death that does not involve my blade is too good for you or your people. I want to see the life fade from your eyes with my blade in your chest."

"I think I'm in love with a samurai." Hugh said.

"I have told you; I am no samurai." Hinata reminded him.

"You have their spirit, that's for sure." Hugh looked back at Sykes. "And his way sounds nice as well since you don't seem interested in stopping what you are doing."

Sykes brought his hands up plaintively. "How can I stop it? It's a system-wide thing. Everyone does it."

"Not everyone." Hugh said. "There are entire cities on Venus where it's not done. Lots of asteroids as well. It's not everyone."

"Dogmatists." Sykes snapped, then his eyes got large. "I mean…"

"You will speak to the… council? Senate? Damn, I didn't look up what they are called. Representatives?"

"Magistrates. Sections of towns have a magistrate; each colony or planet has a governor."

"How very Roman of you." Hugh said. "So who's the Emperor? That was never mentioned."

"There isn't one. Not anymore. In fact," He became almost conversational in his tone. "We are now a republic with each Magistrate getting a share of two hundred votes determined by population. A secretary is appointed every month to chair a meeting if one is required and to tally votes. There is no one person in charge of anything. It's far more peaceful that way."

"And with Mars being the largest concentration of Humans." Hugh glanced at Hinata again. "Besides Earth, that is, where Mars goes, the rest follow."

"Well, yes. Of course."

Hugh stared at the man.

"This isn't an overnight thing." Sykes said after a long moment. "You have to at least realize that."

"I understand that getting people back home will take time." Hugh said. "But... no more ships will be coming to Earth to get more. An immediate quarantine of Earth is definitely doable. At least by Mars now. And as you said, the other cities will follow your lead."

"Yes." Sykes said as he sat up straighter in the chair. "Yes, that is what we will have to do, I suppose." He glanced at the door again.

"You expecting someone? An important meeting or something?" Hugh asked.

"You wouldn't understand." Sykes said.

The door burst open and four armed men charged into the room.

"You think you're so smart!" Sykes said. "Tiberius is my code word for security! Hah!" He pointed at Hugh. "You're an idiot and I'll see you in a cage for THE REST OF MY LIFE AND THE LIVES OF MY CHILDREN'S CHILDREN!"

Hinata took two steps and swung his blade in a broad arc, cutting Governor Sykes' ear cleanly off. "Feel my blade, Akuma!"

Sykes grabbed the side of his head as blood poured down it, he fell to the floor, screaming and thrashing.

Hugh rushed the lead two men. They already had their rifles raised. Thanks to their helmets and visors, he couldn't tell where they were looking. "Hinata, get down!" He shouted as he charged into the front two at an incredible speed, knocking them to the side. He was trying to reach the door to close it before more security came in. One of the men behind the front pair fired at Hugh, hitting him in the chest four times, knocking him to the floor.

"Assailant down." He said cooly.

"Hugh-san!" Hinata shouted as he raised his blade.

"Drop it." The man pointed his weapon at Hinata. "Drop it or die." He turned his head slightly to the man beside him. "Get your cuffs. Simmons, Kilpatrick, you okay?"

The two men on the ground got to their feet slowly.

"Yes, Sir," Kilpatrick said. "I've never seen anyone move that fast. Stinking Venusian genetics."

Simmons picked up his rifle where he had dropped it. "I'm good too."

"I said drop the blade." The man said to Hinata again. "Cuff him, Warrens."

"Roger, Chief." Warrens said. He reached behind his back and took out a pair of steel handcuffs. All four stepped past Hugh and advanced on Hinata.

Hugh quietly stood behind the four men.

"Oh, perhaps we should discuss this." Hinata saw him stand. "Before it is too late."

"It's already too late." The Chief said. "You stupid primitive."

Hugh slowly pushed the door shut. It clacked as the lock reengaged.

The Chief turned to look. "What?"

Hugh lurched forward and grabbed the Chief and Warrens by their helmets then banged them together. The two men fell unconscious.

Kilpatrick and Simmons started to raise their weapons when Hinata charged them. "Shini!" He shouted. (Die).

The men turned back toward Hinata as Hugh reached them. Like the other two, Hugh banged their helmets together hard, incapacitating them.

"Tiberius, lock the door." Hugh said. He figured that even if it was a request for security, it would still be a command the AI would follow. And with security already present, more might not actually come.

"Complying." The deep male voice said as the door's mechanism clacked.

"Nicely done, Hugh-san." He gestured at the door. "It will be a long fight to the elevator box, I think, but I am with you." He held his sword at the ready. "Let us go before more show up."

"We're not going out that way." Hugh moved to the governor. He had stopped screaming and the blood had slowed. "Remember what I said to you that I could do, Governor Sykes. It is a distinct possibility for your city and all of Mars."

Sykes looked at the four holes in Hugh's shirt. They were stained with blood but weren't bleeding. "What?"

A banging on the door made all three look in that direction.

"Put that sword away, Hinata." Hugh said.

"What? We are surrendering?"

"We are leaving." Hugh corrected.

"Hai." Hinata wiped his blade on the Governor's jacket, cutting it as he did.

"You won't get away with this." Sykes said.

Hugh turned to look at Governor Sykes, his eyes flashing to red. "If anyone tries to stop us from leaving, I will infect every single one of them. Armed, hungry vampires is what you will be dealing with. And if you try and warn your people that there's a vampire on the loose on Mars, they'll all think you're crazy."

Sykes glared back at him. "Unlock door!"

As the door clacked open, Hugh grabbed Hinata and spun him around, bear hugging him from behind.

"Hugh-san, I am to be your shield? That is not honorable."

"Stay calm." Hugh said as he picked him off the floor and started running toward the cracked window.

"Oh, no, no no!" Hinata shouted. "Use me as a shield instead!"

"Stay calm." Hugh repeated.

Right before the door burst open and three armed men entered, the two of them crashed through the glass.

Thirty

Abigail looked around the large common area. The fire was still large and blazing, casting light onto the seats three rows back. It was later in the evening and everyone with a family had gone home for dinner and conversation. There were several other couples spread out around the fire but they were focused on each other. It had been decided that the fire pit was adequately public that chaperones were not needed for young couples who were courting, so there was often a dozen different couples, and sometimes quartets sitting and chatting or playing games.

As usual, Abigail sat alone. While she had many friends that she spoke with, they were all married and were home with their husbands and children at this time of night. She looked up at Mars- it was a red speck in a dark sky and let out a sigh.

"May I join you?"

Abigail startled as she was brought out of her thoughts.

"Oh, I'm sorry." Eli said as he patted her shoulder. "I thought you heard me come up."

Abigail smiled. "No, sorry; I was… thinking."

Eli smiled back at her. "I am sorry."

The pair stared at each other for a long moment.

"Oh! Yes please, sit." She gestured beside her on the long wooden bench.

"Ahh.." Eli eased himself onto the bench. He looked up at well. "Mars?"

"It's on my mind." Abigail sighed. "You know, I prayed and prayed that God would bring Gideon back to me. I did not know how it could happen, but I still prayed that it would." She shrugged. "Perhaps they were done with whatever they were doing and were just returning him home. Or perhaps they decided keeping people away from their families was wrong. Or... I don't know... he just came home."

"You didn't expect it to be someone like Hugh."

Abigail nodded. "Not someone like Hugh?" She looked at Mars again. "I never expected *anyone* to have a hand in his return besides Gideon himself, or his captors. I am not sure I want to know what is even going on up there with him right now. But really, I am no longer concerned about it because it's not my doing."

"Oh?" Eli was surprised by Abigail's change of attitude.

Abigal nodded. "It is like Brother Elam said at a service last month; 'If you can praise God when things go well for you, you should also praise Him when they do not. Because God is in charge of all things."

"That is indeed true." Eli nodded.

"So the fact that my prayers have been answered about Gideon coming home is what I should be thankful for." She looked at Eli. "The details are God's business."

"I suppose that's..."

"Because," Abigail held up her hand, fingers extended and brought each one down as she spoke: "It was not me that brought the Gatherers here. It was not me that had them take Gideon after we had been married just two weeks. It was not me that guided Hugh's life putting him in the position where he was frozen. It was not me that brought Hugh to this town." She waggled her thumb. "And it was not me that changed Hugh's attitude to have him even want to go to Mars to try and get Gideon." She made a fist and shook it at him. "No. This is all God's doing and it will go according to His plan. No one can say otherwise to me. *No one.*"

"And no one will, Sister Abigail." Eli smiled. While he was fairly certain she would not hit him, he had been amused to see her punch other people -males that is- when they said something contrary to what her opinion was. While it was only to the arm or shoulder, and never really in anger- the elders were still not pleased with this habit. He brought up his fists as well. "Heaven help them if they do."

"Are you teasing me, Brother Eli?" Abigail put her hands on her lap.

Eli shook his head. "No, not at all. In fact, I am very happy with your attitude; it is healthy. It really is all up to God what happens."

The pair looked at the red planet for a long moment.

"Do you think they will return tomorrow?" Abigail said softly. "While I do not want to rush God, I am a little… anxious that His plans may not happen at the speed I would like."

"That is often the case." Eli patted his thighs. "But you know what we should do in the meanwhile?"

Abigail looked at him.

"Give your home a sound cleaning and sprucing up for the impending return of Gideon."

"Are you suggesting I do not keep a tidy home." Abigail's eyes got large.

"No, I do not. But a fresh coat of paint and any repairs that need done would be a nice welcome for Gideon. I think that while arriving home will be a grand day, having to do chores the very next would not be as pleasant. If we can give him a week or two off to readjust to life at home, we should." He smiled. "Consider it a second honeymoon."

"Oh." Abigail smiled. "I think that would be nice. The gate is sagging a little and the rugs could use a beating."

Eli stood. "Then tomorrow morning I will ask for volunteers to make a quick pass of your home to mend anything that needs mending and to help carry out the rugs to get them beaten. I am sure there will be far more volunteers than tasks."

Abigail stood as well and hugged Eli. "That will be nice." She let go and backed up a step. "Because he will be arriving shortly. I am sure the rescue is taking place without incident."

"How could it not?" Eli raised his hand plaintively.

Thirty-One

"Hugh-san!" Hinata screamed as he and Hugh crashed through the window pane.

Hugh had turned and ducked his head, shielding Hinata as he hit the cracked window with his shoulders. Thanks to the lower gravity, the pair sailed far out from the window as shards of glass started to fall to the ground almost four hundred feet below.

Hinata reached back and grabbed Hugh's shirt. "You kill us both!"

"Calm down." Hugh twisted putting Hinata below him. He concentrated on gliding toward a building that was over a half mile away- it was several stories shorter than the one they had just jumped out of and it seemed to have a garden on the roof, which would make for a softer landing than the metal ones. His first plan was to sail to the ground as close to the ship as possible, the building seemed like a better option since he had never tried to glide a full mile.

Hinata looked down. "You can *fly*? Soratobu akuma!" (Flying devil)

"I don't know what a Soratobu is, but I'm no devil." Hugh said. "Now keep quiet."

"You can fly!"

Hugh concentrated on the building he was trying to reach. "No, I can't."

"I do not mean to call you untruthful, Kyūketsuki, but we are flying right now." Hinata pointed down. "The glass is falling."

"We are *gliding*." Hugh corrected.

"Gliding?"

"I can't gain height." Hugh explained.

"You are like the flying squirrel then." Hinata said.

Hugh smiled. "Yes. Exactly." The comparison was accurate. "But I really need to concentrate on what I am doing if we are going to reach that nice soft garden on top of that building."

Hinata looked forward. It was a very, very long way to the lone garden-topped building. "Ohh." He said worriedly to himself. He looked down. They actually did not seem to be falling as fast as he had expected. He had hunted flying squirrels when he was younger and while they were called 'flying' they did indeed just glide to the ground or to another branch. If they were high enough, they could glide a long way but it was always in a predictable downward trajectory. Which helped him shoot them with his bow. He could tell that they were also falling as they went forward but by looking sideways he could tell that it was at a much slower rate. "We fall very slow, Hugh." He said softly, feeling that Hugh had obviously mastered this skill with how it was going and just was humble about it. "You have great skill."

"It is more thanks to the low gravity on this planet than my skill." Hugh said. Even so, he was now worried he would overshoot the rooftop. He looked past it; there were several other buildings but they had rounded roofs or worse, were much taller than his intended target. He tried to concentrate on moving lower, letting more air pass by him. He did this knowing that aerodynamics had nothing at all to do with what he was doing, but just because he didn't understand it didn't mean he couldn't do it.

"I do not want to worry you…"

"What, Hinata, what is it?" Hugh snapped as his concentration lapsed yet again.

"It is just that you… glide so well, I am now thinking we may miss that nice garden entirely. That larger building behind it seems to be our target now."

"Well maybe I'll just let you go and see how not having to hold a conversation helps my flying."

"I thought we were gliding, Hugh-san." Hinata said. "But at this height, I do not wish to argue the point with you."

Hugh shook his head. During the short interaction, they had in fact dropped down and the rooftop once again seemed within their trajectory. It was now less than a quarter of a mile away- even though they were not dropping quickly, they still were moving at a very fast twenty miles an hour. "Okay, when we get there I'm going to let you go. You're going to need to tuck and roll."

"Tuck and roll, Hugh-san? What is a tuck?"

Hugh frowned; it was hard to concentrate on flying at the same time as speaking. "Fold up in the middle like you are going to tumble over."

"Yes, I understand tumbling. I will be ready." He pulled his knees up to his chest in preparation for being dropped.

Even though there was a much thicker atmosphere inside the dome than outside, Hinata's position did not seem to make any sort of difference aerodynamically. Hugh swooped down as they reached the leading edge of the building. It was about three hundred feet across. Whenever he had glided before, he had just gotten closer and closer to the ground then tried to land while running. Often, he would just tumble and then get to his feet. Landing was something he had in no way mastered. "Okay, here we go…. Now!" he let go of Hinata while moving closer to ten miles an hour.

Hinata grabbed his knees as if he were cannonballing into a pool then crashed through three rows of plants. When he got through the last one, he popped to his feet ready for action but there was no one in the rooftop garden.

Hugh had not been looking at him because he was concentrating on his own landing. He positioned his legs in mid stride and reached out with a toe. When it hit, he pushed off and brought his other leg down, landing in a full sprint. After a dozen strides, he skidded to a stop. "Hinata?" He looked around.

"Hai! Where to now?" Hinata jogged over to Hugh. "Your landing was much better than mine."

"Usually they are a lot messier." Hugh admitted. He spotted the elevator that led down from the roof. "There, an elevator. Let's go. They're going to be right on us." He looked back toward the building they had started in but it was too far away to make out any details. While he had many superior abilities, long-distance sight was not one of them.

He could only see well at night if he had changed. "Go, go, go!" He said as he started for the small square building.

"I am right behind you." Hinata said.

Thirty-Two

"I don't care what you believe, Sergeant!" Governor Sykes roared at the head security guard. "They went out that window!"

After they had entered and found the room empty, the three security guards' stress level dropped considerably. After they tended their four knocked-around comrades and discovered they were all uninjured, they became downright aloof. A lively banter had started between them as often happened among soldiers.

"Out the window huh?" Said the Sergeant. "What'd you see, Chief?" He asked the man he just helped up.

"One guy, really fast." He shook his head. "Augmented so probably North Venusian. And another one, Asian. Not as fast."

"He was more than fast," Sykes said. "He…" He was unsure how much he should tell just a rank-and-file soldier. "Changed when he attacked me," he said vaguely as he looked away.

"Oh, one of those." The Chief nodded at the Sergeant. "Berserker. Seen them before, Sergeant?"

The Sergeant shook his head. "No Chief, but I hear they're tough ones. Still, they'll go down like all the rest. Just takes a few more rounds is all."

"Berserkers?" Now Sykes was unsure about what Hugh had told him. "I've never heard of them."

"It's called fluid genetics." The Chief explained. "They are able to change on the fly. Venusian tech."

"Venusian tech," the Sergeant repeated. "Hate that stuff. Unnatural is what that is."

"But…" Now Sykes was curious. "You shot him four times."

"Body armor." The Chief rapped his knuckles against his own body armor. "Mil-spec is 'one size fits all' so it's bulky; civilian-spec is custom made. You can wear it under a shirt and not have it show. Lots of businessmen wear them. Criminals too. Light and comfortable." He shook his head. "If we suspected, we'd have head-shot him."

"He could fly."

"We all can." The Sergeant interjected. "Arrestors." Now he patted his chest.

"He wasn't wearing one." Sykes said.

"Oh, he was if he was flying." The Sergeant said. "Guaranteed."

"Again, civilian gear is a lot smaller since it's tailored for one person." The Chief explained. "I grab my arrestor from the same stack that some fat slob from the finance office would."

The Sergeant looked at the men by the window. "What do you see out there?"

One of the second set of men was standing at the opening looking down. "Don't see them, Sergeant. Just locals down there. Gawking as usual." He leaned out and spit. "Look out below!"

The other man at the window grabbed him by the back of his armor and jostled him toward the gaping wide opening.

"Quit screwing around, Chase!" The first said as he grabbed the sides of the window frame.

"You're wearing your arrestor." Chase said as he patted his friend on his shoulder. "Besides, I'd have been right behind you, Phil."

Phil turned to look at Chase. "Yeah, because otherwise I'd ride you for a month for not jumping too."

"You know it." Chase laughed. He slapped his friend's shoulder.

"Case in point; we're all wearing one, Governor," The Sergeant said.

"What?"

Chase patted his shoulder. "Good for almost a quarter mile. More if you're not as heavy as Phil here." He slapped his cohort on the back. "Am I right?"

"A quarter mile? What good is that?" Sykes asked.

"It gets you out of the kill zone in an ambush." The Chief pointed at the window. "Or off a rooftop."

Governor Sykes looked at the window as well. Suddenly it was all easily explainable. Vampires indeed.

"Or out of some gal's apartment in a pinch." Phil said.

"Never get caught just in your socks and underwear." Chase added

"Right." Phil said with a chuckle. "So everything is copacetic, Gov'. Good to go even."

"My damned ear was cut off!" The Governor howled. "What do you plan on doing about this person, no matter what they are, Chief!?"

"What do you see, Corporal Jenkins?" Chief asked. His voice was calm and professional. "Got anything?"

Corporal Phil Jenkins eyed the thermal icon on the head's up display in his helmet. With the day's computer-controlled, mild westerly wind, the heat signatures from arrestors would be visible for at least half an hour. "Nothing on thermal. Just regular cool air out there." He panned around the entire area around the building. "Nothing. Weird." He looked at the Governor, then his Sergeant, then the Chief. "I got nothing. They've ghosted."

Phil gave a nod. "I think we're done here, Sir. If you want my opinion."

"Get that ear looked at, Governor. You've probably got another twenty minutes for them to put it back on so don't lollygag." The Chief said. He brought his hand over his head and spun it in a circle. "I'm rolling in ten. Load up or you're walking."

"To go after him, right?"

The Chief looked at the Governor. "Do you know which way he went, since we can't spot them?"

"They both flew toward that apartment building." Sykes pointed. "Over there."

"But there's no exhaust trail." Corporal Jenkins interjected. "I'm sorry Governor, there just isn't."

"You said that one of them could fly. Now they both can?" The Chief asked.

"No. I mean yes. I mean… one was carrying the other. He grabbed him from behind and then jumped out the window with him."

Chase let out a laugh. "Oh, sorry, Chief." He looked down at the floor.

"Now I'm rolling in nine." Chief said. With that he turned and marched out of the room.

"But." Governor Sykes said. The two men by the window quickly moved after their Chief, ignoring him. Sykes frowned. "Sergeant?"

"We've got our own transportation, Governor." The Sergeant said. "And like the Chief said, you need to get that ear dealt with ASAP."

"This is outrageous!" Governor Sykes went back to shouting. "Two men come into my office, attack four of your own, assault me, then escape and you don't care? I'll be speaking with General Sampson about this!"

"I'll make sure he gets our feeds right away." The Sergeant said. He let out a sigh. Even with the General getting everyone's body camera feed to show they had done nothing wrong; it was still an incident in the Governor's office. And the Governor's ear had been cut off, there was no denying that. "We'll do a sweep of the surrounding two blocks on our way back to ops and question the locals. Swing by that apartment building even."

"Fine, fine." Governor Sykes said. The explanations the soldiers gave did seem reasonable, more reasonable than an actual vampire existing. But even so, he realized that they couldn't explain why there were no exhaust signatures from the window. It was infuriating because Hugh was correct; he just couldn't say there was a vampire loose on Mars. But a Venusian berserker was definitely plausible. Once he had Hugh behind glass, he could have him examined properly to see what the truth actually was. "Just fine; you go do that." He added, not confident the Marines would make anything more than a cursory search. Of course, he did have his own personal security contingent that would work as diligently as he paid them to.

"Great," The Sergeant said, feeling like he had smoothed things out with the Governor. "Let's roll, gentlemen." He turned and walked to the door. When he got there he abruptly stopped, Chase and Phil almost bumped into him. "Don't forget what the Chief said; there's a time limit on that ear going back on."

"Even with one ear I heard you the first three times!" The Governor shouted. There was a medical facility on the first floor of the building so he would be there in plenty of time. He reached down and picked up his ear, seething from not only the pain but by the fact that some primitive had come into his office, demanded things of him, lied to his face, and assaulted him. It was outrageous. "Now get going!"

"Roger that, Governor." The Sergeant replied, now planning on just taking a quick look around so he and his team would be finished before the end of their shift. "We're on it. Let's go." He gestured out the door and marched off, his two subordinates right behind.

Governor Sykes contacted his head of security as he went to the clinic to have the matter handled professionally.

Thirty-Three

Hugh pressed the button calling the elevator. "Okay, once we get down, we need to get a couple of blocks over; then straight down a half mile. That's where the ship is sitting."

"Hugh-san, I understand you are much more experienced with these things than I."

"But." Hugh offered.

"Getting into the elevator thing does not seem wise to me." Hinata added.

Hugh looked around the rooftop. "Why's that?"

"If they have seen us flying here, then there may be people waiting for us when the doors to the small room… the elevator opens. Then we will be trapped." Hinata stepped around the steel square. "It is not that far to the ground. Can we fly to where the ship is from here or do you tire using your gifts?"

Hugh smirked. He had never thought of any of his abilities, or his condition for that matter, as a 'gift'. "No, I don't get tired gliding." He said. "As far as I know anyway. This is actually the highest height I have ever jumped from." The elevator chimed indicating it had arrived. As the doors opened, Hugh crouched down, prepared to deal with any security forces inside. "Huh." He stood. "Empty."

"The trap usually is until the prey goes in." Hinata said. He had walked back over to look at the elevator. "Then it is too late to do anything but look surprised and then get eaten."

Hugh let out a long breath. "You make a good point." The doors started to close so he reached out and stopped them from doing so. "Keep your hand here so the doors don't close." He pointed with his free hand. "Don't let them close."

Hinata put his hand beside Hugh's then braced his feet. "I am ready."

"It won't be hard to keep open." Hugh explained. "They are designed so that if someone's arm or leg is in the way it won't close injuring them." He jogged over to the plants Hinata had crushed when he landed. There were several buckets there.

"What are you doing?" Hinata asked. He startled as the doors tried to close. He was surprised that with very little pressure, they opened completely again. "Hah! That is most interesting."

Hugh took two large buckets and scooped up dirt with them.

"Are we stealing dirt, Hugh? There is plenty back in my village."

Hugh ignored him and filled four buckets. He quickly carried two over and put them in the elevator then returned for the other two.

"Hugh-san?" Hinata tried again.

When Hugh put the other two buckets in the elevator he turned to Hinata. "They might have a way of telling if we are in there or not. The weight of the dirt will make them believe we are." He stepped into the elevator.

"Hugh-san, it is a trap!"

"Yes, I think it might be." Hugh pressed the buttons for the bottom ten floors. "But this will keep them waiting for us at the bottom to give us a little time."

"I do not care that you argue with me about it; I say you are a devil." Hinata smiled. He grabbed the door with both hands when it tried to close again. "A cunning devil."

"That I will accept." Hugh stepped out of the elevator. "Okay, let's go."

"Hai!" Hinata watched the doors close with a smile on his face. "Their trap has only caught dirt. Hah! Feast on THAT!"

"Let's go." Hugh jogged to the edge of the roof. He could see the row of ships just under a half mile away. Thanks to his experience with his most recent flight, he knew he could reach them even being a good ten stories lower. He turned on his communication device. "Isaac, are you there?"

"Hugh! Where are you?" Isaac asked nervously.

"We are on our way back. You thinking of leaving me. *Again?*"

"Oh… well, no. Of course not." Isaac said unconvincingly.

"We are less than ten minutes out. I want you to start the pre-flight steps from the list I gave you."

"Right." Isaac replied.

"Don't take off, Isaac. Just run through the list to the one that says 'start engines' but don't do anything after that. Okay?"

"Okay." Isaac replied. "So I start the engines or stop before that one?"

Hugh shook his head. "Do not start the engines. Stop before that step."

"Okay, I will start right now. Not starting the engines… starting the list."

Now Hinata shook his head.

"Good. And don't open the door for anyone until I get there." Hugh said.

"Oh." Isaac replied.

"What do you mean 'oh'?"

"Well, Gideon went outside earlier."

"For what?" Hugh scowled. "Get him back inside *and keep him there!* And start the take-off procedures. There are people looking for us. Dangerous people. I don't have time to run in circles looking for him!"

"I'm sure he is already inside," Isaac explained. "He just went out for a little bit. He's back now. I'm sure he is."

"Good. Stay put and start the take-off procedure." Hugh closed the radio link. "Just great. I find him then he goes wandering off." He thought back to the take-off routine; it took him about five minutes to go through it which is why he wanted Isaac to start it before he got there. In fact, he should have called Isaac when he first landed on the roof. Now it seemed they would be sitting defenseless on the ground as he loaded telemetry and calculated their take off trajectory, among a dozen other things.

"These Amish will get you killed, Hugh. They are reckless and unaware of the dangers around them." Hinata said as the pair walked to the edge of the building. "It is a dangerous combination; children have this same issue."

"They are very innocent people." Hugh shrugged. "Hardworking and dedicated, but innocent."

"That is why you feel you must protect them." Hinata said. "Like children?"

"It's complicated." Hugh replied.

"Or perhaps they are pets?" Hinata chuckled.

"Ready?"

"I am ready to fly again. Twice in one day! And I will not talk until we get there this time." Hinata stepped between the edge of the building and Hugh- his toes were over the edge. "Junbi kanryō." (Ready to go)

Hugh looked where Hinata was standing. It struck him that this man whom he had only recently met now trusted him with his life. It was a striking display of how much he had changed in a short amount of time for people to be this comfortable around him. He thought about what Hinata had said; he had put himself at risk for the people in Anchorage. But that was what one did with family, wasn't it? The change in his priorities was confusing and he decided he needed some time alone to decide how he wanted to live from now on. He frowned; his life was simpler when he just lived day to day but it was a very singular existence and there wasn't much security in it. Sleep, hunt, move on- relying only on himself. Now he had people that interacted with him daily. And he didn't worry about sleeping; there were people in town who would make sure he was safe the entire day. And people routinely invited him into their homes- even the ones that were aware of his condition. It was a drastic change in lifestyle.

"Hugh-san, I said I would not speak until we got there, but now it seems it may take a long time since we are not moving."

"Not moving, huh?" Hugh shoved Hinata off the roof.

Hinata spun his arms backwards trying to maintain his balance but was unable to. "You devil!" He shouted as he fell into open air.

Thirty-Four

Governor Sykes clenched the armrests of the chair as the doctor worked on his ear. While the procedure was straightforward, it was very painful. Especially since the Governor had declined general anesthetic so he could speak to his head of security with a clear head.

"Hold still." The doctor said. "Or you'll have a crooked ear. They'll call you Lopsy."

Sykes glowered at the man. "They will call me *Governor.*"

The doctor shrugged as he held the thread taunt and snipped it close to the skin with a pair of scissors. He put down the needle. Four sutures were holding the ear in place until the skin cells connected the ear to the man's scalp again. "I didn't vote for you."

A man peeked into the examination room. "Is it safe to come in?"

"I'm not contagious," The doctor said.

"Come in, Rex," Governor Sykes said to his head of security. "We're almost done here."

Rex stepped in and closed the door. "What's going on?"

"I just reattached his ear." The Doctor said. "It should heal just fine."

Governor Sykes scowled. "He wasn't asking for a medical update." He glanced at the doctor then back to Rex. "A guy broke into my office, made all sorts of outlandish demands, then cut off my ear."

"Building security get him?"

The doctor picked up an applicator. "Hold still."

Governor Sykes ignored the doctor and shook his head. "No, they went out the window."

"They?" Rex stepped to the side and sat on a rolling stool. "Now it's *they* all of a sudden?"

"There were actually two of them. One was in charge, the other was some sort of loudmouth lackey." He gestured at his ear. "With a sword of all things."

"I see." Rex nodded. "So they attacked you then suicided? Sounds like the separatists from Venus. You know; those 'Sovereign Venus' idiots."

Governor Sykes shook his head again. "No, they weren't SoVus."

"If you don't hold still," the Doctor interrupted, "I'll just kick you out now and let that thing go septic right on the side of your head."

"And they're not dead either." Governor Sykes looked over. "Sorry, Doc. I'll hold still." He looked straight ahead even though he didn't like the man. The fact of the matter was that he only had about ten more minutes before the tissue in his ear started to die and there wasn't enough time to go to another clinic. "Go ahead."

"Fine then." The Doctor said. He removed the cover from the applicator exposing a long plastic needle. "This is going to sting." He said as he hesitated. "Nothing I can do about it either without general anesthetic."

"Do it." Sykes gripped the armrests again.

"Not dead? Did they have arrestors or parachutes?"

Governor Sykes glanced at the doctor without moving his head. "No. Maybe. It's complicated. The bottom line is they said they were from Earth but the one displayed Venusian extremist tech. Fluid genetics I think the Chief called it."

"Primitives?" Rex said. "And they broke into your office?" He shook his head. "No; Venusian extremists is more likely. Wait, they were Berserkers as well?"

"You've heard of them?"

"Sure have. Berserkers? You're lucky you're still alive." Rex shuddered. "Augmented physical abilities and disabled moral compasses."

The doctor inserted the thin plastic needle -more an applicator than anything else- between the Governor's scalp and his ear. He squeezed the plunger and began applying a gel of T-cells and pain killers between the two. He worked his way around the ear until the gel oozed out the edges. "The edges will dry to form an airtight seal in about thirty minutes. Your cells will start growing right away in the meanwhile. In case you don't know, keep this dry for forty-eight hours and don't go swimming for a week." He put down the tube. "And avoiding any altercations should go without saying." He turned to a small table with instruments on it. "Let me give you another antibiotic; no telling what was on that blade."

"Thanks." Sykes said. He continued to Rex: "I want these two found and brought to me. Actually the Japanese one doesn't matter as much. The Caucasian one does. He seems knowledgeable so he might be property of a scientist or he's at least well aware of Venusian tech. Either way, him I definitely want alive."

"Can do." Rex replied. "Do you know where they're staying?"

"No idea. They have to have some place around here. It's not like they could fly out of here."

"There's that big dome in the way," the Doctor said as he injected the governor with a pneumatic syringe. "There, you could swallow a dead rat and you'd be fine."

Sykes looked at the Doctor. "Is that it?"

The Doctor nodded. "Yeah, but I want you to stay here for the half-hour to make sure the seal is good before you leave. The first thirty minutes is critical."

"Find them, Rex. I'll be in my office in an hour. You can give me an update there."

"You got it, boss." Rex stood. "I'll go see who's who in the zoo."

"Oh no you won't!" The Doctor interrupted. "You're going home for the next forty-eight hours. You'll sit around and do a lot of nothing in the nice clean air of your home. That's what you're going to be doing!"

"There are things I need to get done." Sykes replied.

"You have a staff to do that. If they can't handle two days without you, you need to fire every last one of them." The Doctor gestured at Rex. "And I'm sure he can call you *at home* later to tell you what he found out. You need to sit in a nice, clean, filtered environment and not be walking around outside in the dust." Even with a dome over the entire city, there was always a fine layer of red dust in the air; no amount of filtration seemed capable of keeping it out. Inside a home, better and more expensive filtration systems were able to. "*Home.* That's an order."

"Fine, Doctor. I'll go home."

"I'll see what I can find out and give you a call later this afternoon." Rex said as he pointed at the doctor. "I'll call him at home."

"Good." The Doctor said. "Now go away." He shoo'ed Rex off. "Off with you!"

With that Rex left the office.

Governor Sykes started to get out of the chair. "Okay, I'll just head home."

"No you won't. Weren't you paying attention? You need to sit here for thirty minutes so that if that ear isn't sealed all the way around I can fix it. The last thing you need is sand or even air getting in there." He reached out and touched the reattached ear. "It's already getting good color and is feeling warmer. We need to make sure it keeps going that way."

"For someone you didn't vote for, you sure seem to care about me a lot."

"Oh, you'll be in my next commercial as a satisfied customer." The Doctor smirked. "A high-level government employee is always a good endorsement."

"What? I'm not going to appear in any commercial."

The Doctor shrugged. "Who said anything about appearing? I'm just going to say that I treated you after a heinous, debilitating terrorist attack. Our beloved Governor's ear successfully reattached with no complications after being maliciously attacked by Venusian Berserkers." He gave a curt nod. "Yeah, that sounds good. Makes you sound heroic as well, I should think."

"Fair enough." Conceded Sykes. If anything, the fact that he was able to survive an attack could be used in his reelection campaign. "I'll sit here for thirty then catch a ride home."

"Good." The Doctor pointed at a monitor. "Catch up on the news and I'll check back in on you in twenty minutes." Without waiting for a reply, he turned and left.

With a scowl, Sykes turned on the Martian News Network to see if anything about the attack was being reported.

It was- annoyingly along with videos people had sent in of a man flying while carrying another man. "I hope you're watching that, Chief." Sykes said sourly.

Thirty-Five

Just as Hinata's feet left the ledge, Hugh jumped after him.

"You devil!" Hinata shouted again.

Hugh glided closer and grabbed Hinata after only about twenty feet of free fall.

"Oh, you devil." Hinata said again, but less angry now that Hugh had grabbed him from behind.

Hugh laughed. "You looked so comfortable right there at the edge."

"I am not afraid of heights. I climb trees and cliffs when I hunt. Falling is another matter however." Hinata looked ahead. "We will reach the ship?"

Hugh looked as well- the distance was definitely manageable. Whether Isaac and Gideon had the ship ready when they got there was another story entirely. "Yes, we will make it there."

Hinata looked down. "There are people watching us, did you know this?"

Hugh had considered that issue when he first jumped through the window. He had decided that by the time the glass had hit the pavement far below, he would be out of the pedestrian's line of sight behind another building when they looked up. Now they were much lower and thanks to flying toward a landing area that was at the end of a major street, there were no buildings shielding them. Hugh saw that several people pointed as he sailed by fairly slowly. While they had seen people fly wearing jet packs or parachutes, someone flying apparently of their own account was completely different. "We won't be answering any questions from anyone when we land."

"Hai!"

"Or killing people," Hugh reminded.

"Ahh, wakatta." (Okay)

Hugh ignored him and returned to concentrating on his flight- he still needed to make sure they made it to the landing zone- inside the high perimeter wall. He went over the preflight routine in his head in case Isaac hadn't started it. He was not familiar enough with the process to skip any steps, which was frustrating.

As the pair finally sailed over the perimeter wall of the landing zone, they were a mere twenty feet above the ground. By then there were several pedestrians following their movement down the street. When they got to the high perimeter wall, Hugh dropped down out of their line of sight. He was relieved to see there was no one waiting around for them inside the area.

"Get ready!" Hugh said as he dropped behind the wall, "here goes." He let go of Hinata when he was about eight feet off the ground and moving forward at a pace equal to a quick run.

Hinata hit the ground with flexed legs and rolled over twice before popping to his feet. He drew his short sword and pivoted around looking for any would-be attackers.

Hugh sailed a few feet past him and landed in a stumbling walk, ending up having to put his hands on the ship to stop himself from running into it.

"Nicely done, Hugh-san!" Hinata said.

The engines of the ship whined to life, making them both look.

"What? They are leaving us!" Hinata said. "Devil Amish!"

Hugh chuckled. "That's something I never expected to hear." He looked at the ship. However he had definitely told Isaac not to start the engines. He tapped his communication device. "Isaac?"

"Excuse me!" A man said as he walked quickly toward the pair. "Who are you and what exactly are you two doing?"

"Who me?" Hugh asked as he pointed at himself.

"Yes, you!" The man pointed at him. "You. Specifically you."

"What am I doing?" Hugh asked, stalling. "I'm just standing here." He pointed at the ground. "Specifically here." The engines whined louder.

"Who are you?" The man stepped toward Hugh. "That's what I want to know."

"Hugh?" Isaac said in Hugh's earpiece. "What do you need?"

"Isaac?"

"You seem unsure that is your name." The man narrowed his eyes at Hugh.

"Oh, no; someone was talking in my ear. I'm Leroy. I'm piloting the Knik Anchorage for my brother Carl. Carl Nunis." Hugh jerked a thumb at the ship. "We were just dropping off a shipment and now we're heading home." He tapped his communicator. "Isaac, just a moment."

"Sure. I'll just need to see your flight plan, *Carl*." The man said unbelievingly.

"Absolutely." Hugh glanced over at Hinata. "Oh, my friend over there has it on him."

Hinata smiled wide. "Oh, I do indeed, Hugh-san." He said as he moved his blade behind his back to hide it.

As the man started to turn to look at Hinata, Hugh hit him in the jaw with a roundhouse punch. It was not very hard because he wasn't sure how strong the bones of a Martian were. If the ones he encountered back on Earth were any indication, they were much softer than an Earthling's bones. Even so, the man staggered back as his eyes rolled up in his head. He fell backward, arms limp at his sides. Hugh rushed at the man.

"Yes! Finish him!" Hinata cheered.

Hugh grabbed the man before he hit the ground with his head completely unprotected. "Isaac, open the hatch! Hinata, you get aboard the ship." He said as he half carried, half dragged the man to the perimeter wall. He sat the man down then leaned him against the wall. "One more safe and sound, Abigail." He said as he turned and jogged to the ship.

Hinata was still standing there watching him. "He is not dead?"

"No! I told you I promised my friend not to kill any Martians."

"You are indeed an honorable man, Hugh." Hinata said.

"Great. Now get on the ship before I kill you!"

"Ahhh." Hinata raised a finger. "You just said you wouldn't kill anyone." He swiveled his finger over to the ship. "The door is not open."

"I said no Martians, you crazy *Earthling*!" Hugh tapped his communicator again. "ISAAC! OPEN THE DOOR!"

Dutifully the door opened.

"Finally!" Hugh grabbed Hinata by the arm and dragged him up the ramp.

"Do not drag me like a pet!" Hinata fought to get loose from Hugh but was unable to. "Do not drag me!" Once they were inside the ship, Hugh let him go. "Oh, that was not honorable at all." He smoothed out his shirt. "Not at all, Hugh-san."

Hugh ignored him as he ran to the cockpit. "Cynthia, secure the main hatch!"

"The main hatch is closing." Cynthia replied in her ever-calm voice.

Hugh pressed the button and entered the cockpit. Isaac and Gideon were both inside- Isaac in the copilot seat and Gideon in the navigator's position. "We are getting out of here." He hopped over the armrest and into the pilot seat. "Where are we on the list?"

"We are ready to take off." Isaac said. "I started the engines when I saw you come over the wall. Just in case." His eyes got large. "Is that man going to be okay?"

"Yes; I just knocked him out." Hugh looked at Isaac. "You loaded a flight plan for Earth?"

"I didn't know how to tell the ship that."

"Okay..." Began Hugh. "So..."

"Then I figured you wouldn't want to go straight back to Earth anyway so I set it for Deimos because the ship said it remembered that flight plan." Isaac continued. "Once we're on the way, we can turn to go to Earth when they're not watching, right?"

Hugh tapped the icon to power the engines to ten percent- plenty to lift off from Mars' gravity; there was no reason to raise any sort of alarms. The unconscious flight officer would be enough of an issue. The display of the landing gear went from red to yellow to green as they stopped supporting the ship. "Lifting off." He tapped another icon. "Hinata, get strapped in."

"Are we going home now?" Gideon asked.

"That's the plan," Hugh replied. He tapped the communication icon. "Flight Operations, this is the Knick Anchorage."

"Go Knick." A bored voice replied.

"Requesting permission to return home." Hugh said. "Time for a beer."

"Seems like you're already up in the air Knick." There was a little more annoyance than boredom in the voice this time. "You in a hurry?"

"Just to get home," Hugh tried. "It's been a long week."

After a moment, the voice said, "Deimos?"

Hugh nodded. "Roger that. I left my flight plan with that guy on the ground."

"Antonelli."

"Didn't get his name, Ops." Hugh cringed. "He was talking to someone else at the time and I didn't want to interrupt the conversation. Old pal or something." He added hoping it would keep anyone from looking for the unconscious man. "Confirming; heading to Deimos."

There was another, much longer pause. Then: "Fine, Knick Anchorage. Sending course for Deimos rendezvous. Got some traffic to avoid so flight time is two hours. Sorry about that; it's the long way around."

"Got it." Hugh said as he tapped the icon accepting the course into his navigation computer. "See you next time."

"Yeah, sure." The voice said, sounding bored once again. "F-O out."

"That was weird." Hugh said.

"What? They don't seem to suspect anything." Gideon said.

"Cynthia, what is the flight time to Deimos from our current position?" Hugh asked.

"Thirty-five minutes." Cynthia replied.

"Oh, that is odd." Isaac said. "They did say there were things to avoid so maybe there are other ships in the way or something?"

"Or something." Hugh said. "Maybe they're sending us on a big loop so they have time to catch us and board us when we land. Or maybe there's other traffic to worry about. I'm going to go with the first one."

"Are you sure they are lying?" Gideon said.

"I don't trust anyone," Hugh replied. "It's why I've lived so long."

Isaac winked at Gideon. "Plus he was frozen in ice for a lot of it."

Hugh glanced at Isaac. "I'm replacing you with Hinata, just so you know."

"What?"

"If I get a sidekick, it'll be him."

Isaac frowned. "Oh, I wasn't trying to make you upset." He nodded at Gideon. "But he was really frozen in a glacier for a really long time."

Hugh just shook his head. "Okay, so here's the plan; once we are on our way to Deimos, I'm going to cut the engines and everything else I can safely turn off. Then we'll run silent for a day. Then we will head back to Earth."

"When you turn off the engines, won't we just stop? Like paddling a canoe?"

"No, Gideon," Hugh replied. "That's not how things work in space; there isn't anything out here to make us slow down. We will just keep going in the same direction, at the same speed we were going. Then I'll change our name to something else, start up the engines and then go to Earth. Once we get there, I'll figure out how to hide the ship there."

Gideon stared at Hugh for a moment as he tried to process what he had just been told. "Okay, I will trust your guidance on this." He looked at Isaac for support. "Yes?"

Isaac stood. "Hugh is trustworthy. Let's go to the back while he works, Brother Gideon."

Gideon stood as well. "We will leave you to it, Brother Hugh."

The pair left the cockpit without another word.

Hugh leaned back in his seat. *Hugh is trustworthy.* The words struck him like a ton of bricks. He had never been called that by anyone, ever. Before the only thing others could trust was that he was about to kill them. Now he was 'trustworthy' and 'Brother Hugh'. "Devil Amish." Was all he could say.

Thirty-Six

Gideon was sitting in the co-pilot seat, playing with the monitors as the ship -now called the *Alba Mons*- cut through the clouds towards Alaska. "I never thought I'd ever see this again." He said.

Hugh nodded but kept his attention on the controls. They had spent a day and a half drifting after leaving Mars on a broad arc around the planet that pointed them back toward Earth. During that time, most all ship functions had been turned off except the food control, life support, and the heaters. According to Cynthia, the ship did not produce enough of an electrical signature to be noticed unless a ship passed within fifty miles of them- and none had. So for all intents and purposes, the *Knick Anchorage* left Mars and once it was a hundred miles away, it disappeared. A hundred thirty million miles away, the *Alba Mons* appeared. Cynthia also confirmed that once the ship was on the ground, all ship functions could be turned off and it would merely look like a large mineral deposit once the reactor had cooled off in three hours. The down side was that it would then take twelve hours to recompress the Oganesson to create a new singularity to then power the ship. "We'll be in Anchorage in about ten minutes." Hugh looked at a readout he had placed on the edge of his control panel. "And it will be four in the afternoon when we land. Sunset will be at eleven."

"I don't know how to thank you." Gideon said.

"You already have." Hugh replied. "A dozen times." At one point, Hugh had remarked that Gideon could thank him by making a bunch of babies, but that had embarrassed Gideon to the point where he didn't speak to Hugh for almost three hours. He really had no better reply. *Hugh is trustworthy.* While that compliment made the entire endeavor worthwhile, he did not want to try and explain why it was so meaningful lest Gideon would think less of him. "I'll do a pass over the town so that they know we are home. It's not like we can call them."

"Call them what?" Gideon asked.

"Exactly." Hugh said. "I mean we have no way of contacting them. This way the people who know about our trip will come to the landing area and gather in a calm, very plain crowd."

"There! There is Anchorage! Just like I remember it." Gideon slapped his hands on his knees. "Oh, this is exciting!"

"Fine then; mostly calm, but definitely plain." Hugh said. He tapped an icon to speak to the rest of the ship. "I'm starting the landing process; you should all sit down and buckle up. Afterall this really is just my second landing."

Gideon looked at Hugh. "What?"

"I learned to fly this machine right before I came to get you."

"*What?*" Gideon's eyes got large as he looked around the cockpit. "I thought you were making a joke."

"I landed on Deimos myself." Hugh continued. "But on Mars, they landed the ship for me." He pointed downward. "This. This right here is my second landing ever."

"Oh dear." Gideon said. He looked at the monitors. "I am really looking forward to seeing Abigail and the others, you know."

"I've got it under control." Hugh said even though he was very nervous. He was sure that even if he completely botched the landing, he would survive the crash, however making it all the way home then killing everyone else aboard would mean that he would have to leave town. Landing well enough that no one got hurt but the ship was destroyed so he no longer had a space craft was also a terrible outcome. This was an all-or-nothing endeavor. "How about we just keep quiet until we're safely on the ground, okay?"

"I will pray silently." Gideon said as he put his head back and closed his eyes. "It will all be just fine; our fate is in your hands."

"Oh man." Hugh tapped an icon lowering the landing gear. Three smaller icons turned green, letting him know they were all working properly. So far. He turned the yoke gently, taking the ship over the town. Worried about getting too low, he passed over it at five hundred feet. Even so, he could see on the monitors that a great many people looked up and pointed as he went by. He hoped that word would be sent to Eli. "Coming about to the landing zone." He said to no one in particular. He slid a lit-up bar downward, reducing the engine output to slow his turn.

The ship slowed as it came over the original landing area; it looked quite large when he was on the ground, now it seemed pitifully small. Hugh pulled back on the yoke to bring the ship into a hover as he watched both the monitor to make sure he was in the middle of the area and the altimeter. He was down to four hundred feet already. The ship was dropping faster than he would have liked so he slid the power bar upward two notches. The numbers indicating feet slowed somewhat. He was at three hundred feet and the numbers were scrolling down quickly. He tapped the engine power bar another time and the numbers slowed yet again.

Hinata opened the door and leaned in. "Are we there? It does not seem that we are moving anymore."

"We are not there yet." Gideon said to him. "But we are close." He pointed at the monitor. "The people are easy to see now."

"Ahh, that is good." Hinata stepped into the cockpit. "Very good. Well done, Hugh-san."

"I agree." Gideon said.

"I always had great confidence in his abilities to return us to Earth."

"I just can't believe that…"

"If you two could keep quiet!" Hugh said as he looked over his shoulder at Hinata. As he did, he pulled the yoke, putting the ship into a sideways slide. "This isn't at all easy and I'm trying to not kill all of you by crashing right in front of everyone in town."

"I am sorry Hugh-san." Hinata said. He sat in the third seat. "I will not interrupt again."

"Hugh?" Gideon said. "Those trees are getting closer."

Hugh looked at the monitor; they had shifted to the far side of the clearing. "Oh man." He twisted the yoke and the ship's sideward motion started in the other direction. "Come on, come on."

The altimeter showed a mere ninety feet now.

The ship moved closer to the center of the clearing, almost where it was sitting when they had taken off a few days ago. As the ship shifted back and forth, the crowd on the ground moved as well to keep their distance.

Hugh watched as the altimeter counted down through the teens and into single digits. The ship hit the ground hard. Hugh looked at the readouts; one of the landing gear was now yellow. "Damn it all." He cursed as he shut down the engines.

"What is wrong, Hugh? We are on the ground." Hinata said. "That is a success."

"One of the landing gear… the feet of the ship got damaged. I was coming down too fast." He let out a long breath. "I'll look at it later. At least we're down."

"Can we get off the ship?" Isaac said over the ship's intercom. "It sure felt like we landed. Or did we hit something?"

Hugh glanced at Gideon

Gideon smirked back at him. "Youth." He said. "Especially a young Isaac." He unbuckled his belt. "But leaving the ship is something I want to do as well." He held up a hand. "It isn't because I am ungrateful you know."

Hugh nodded. "I am sure Abigail is just as anxious to see you." He unbuckled his belt. "So let's go. I'll come back to tend to the ship tonight once everyone is settled back in town."

Gideon stood. "Tend to the ship? The damaged foot?"

"That and I need to move the ship closer to the forest and turn everything off so that it can't be seen from above."

"I will help you with that if you would like," Hinata said. "I have no one to welcome me here."

"Thanks." Hugh said. Having someone on the ground as he moved the ship toward the trees would be helpful.

"You think they will come for us?" Gideon followed Hugh and Hinata to the door and into the back portion of the ship.

"I insulted them by stealing their property and the governor was injured. So yeah, they will definitely come looking for us. Or me, really."

"Stealing is definitely wrong and I am sorry the governor was injured." Gideon frowned. "But I am not anyone's property." He looked at Hugh. "How badly was he hurt?"

"Not bad enough." Hinata said. "He only lost an ear to my blade."

"It's been reattached by now." Hugh said matter-of-factly. He pressed the button cycling the airlock. "Definitely."

"What?" Gideon asked. "How?"

"They were able to do things like that in my time, I am sure it is a much easier procedure now." Hugh said. "But even with his ear healed, his pride isn't. He'll definitely be looking for me and the ship."

The ramp dropped down and the three men looked out into the clear bright day.

"That's a sight for sore…" Hugh was interrupted by Isaac shoving his way past and out of the ship. "Well then." He put his arm on Gideon's shoulder. "You should go say hello now that Isaac has paved the way."

"You're not going?"

"Not until nightfall." Hugh said. "My condition doesn't do well with sunlight."

"Oh. Well… Nightfall?" Gideon looked at Hugh. "Please excuse me, Brother Hugh." Gideon worked his way from under Hugh's arm. "There's someone I need to speak with and I'd really not like to wait until nightfall to do it." He quickly went down the ramp without waiting for a reply.

Hugh smirked. "Such polite folks, these Devil Amish." He crouched down to look out the doorway at Abigail and had to admit, she looked anything but plain. "Good for you, Gideon. Good for you." He took a step back from the airlock -and the sunlit clearing- into the cool blue darkness of the ship. He could have waited until dark to land but decided against delaying just in case anyone had followed them.

"There is almost a tear in my eye from your tenderness, Hugh-san." Hinata said. "I shall wait with you."

"Since you don't know anyone out there, that sounds like a good idea." Hugh looked at him. "I imagine one of the town elders, Eli will be here shortly and I will introduce you. Then we need to get this ship moved out of sight." He smirked. "Plus we need to make sure the townspeople know you're not an Inuit."

Hinata nodded, then got serious. "It is just us now, Hugh. You think we were followed? Because I would follow if these events had happened to me. Followed with a fury."

"They might."

"And does your oath to this woman continue?"

Hugh considered that. He had promised to not kill anyone while getting Gideon home, but now that had been accomplished. It would be easy to say that the promise to not kill was complete. Even so, it now troubled Hugh. "No, not that oath, but I think the people of the town… my friends in the town would think less of me if I did just return to killing anyone and everyone."

"You may not be able to avoid it, Hugh." Hinata replied. "These people will not be coming to talk with you." He tapped the hilt of his sword. "Or the two of us for that matter. It was my blade that loosed that man's ear."

Hugh let out a long breath. "I will do what I need to do to keep the people in town safe. And if that means I need to leave afterwards, then that's what I will do." He looked at Hinata and shrugged. "Ashita wa ashita no kaze ga fuku." (Literally "Tomorrow, tomorrow's wind will blow"; do not worry about the future- things change over time.)

"We will make that wind blow, the two of us!" Hinata smiled wide. "I will call you Kamikaze Hugh!" (Divine Wind)

Hugh shrugged. "Or they might not find us. That is also possible."

"It wouldn't be that difficult to find us, I don't think." Hinata replied.

"If they come, they come."

Hinata put his hands on his weapons. "I welcome their arrival."

Thirty-Seven

"Finally." Governor Sykes said as he turned to face the monitor. "It's been a whole day!"

"Morning, Sam. You feeling better?" Rex replied calmly. "I called yesterday afternoon and Marcia said you were asleep. So I figured you needed to rest."

"For a whole day?" The governor had given up trying to get Rex from calling him by his first name. It was definitely insubordinate behavior but Rex was such a useful asset, he couldn't afford to fire him. Rex had at least stopped calling him by his first name when there were other people around.

Rex shrugged. "It's not like there was anything you could do with the information yesterday evening."

"Fine, fine. What have you found out?" The governor asked. In truth, he had spent most of the previous day sleeping. After the adrenalin wore off, his ear throbbed horribly. So he had overmedicated with his pain pills and slept through what he hoped was the worst of his recuperation. This morning his ear did actually feel better and looked close to normal- if the large sutures and ring of dried goo was ignored.

"Well, thanks to an unconscious flight manager, I think I've got a handle on them."

"An unconscious flight manager?"

"Yeah, an F-M at Gate Five had an altercation with a couple of men." Rex raised a finger. "One of which was Asian. Then the pair got into a ship called the Knick Anchorage."

"The what?"

"It's a fake name; the ship's the Giselle. The man tried to pass himself off as the owner's brother, Carl Nunis. Which led me to the Rollins' home on Deimos. Cy Rollins is missing, presumed dead. Her son is very dead. They found his body early this morning. Along with a very alive security guard who corroborated a lot of my information."

"How does any of this help? So they're on Deimos?"

"Well, Operations did put them into an approach to Deimos. But then they went dark before they got there."

"So what you're saying is you lost them."

Rex shrugged. "I figured they weren't actually going there since the son was killed there hours earlier so…"

"Yeah, smart move." Governor Sykes interrupted. "Brilliant."

"*So.*" Rex pressed on, "Based on their descriptions, I searched for ships heading to Venus and Earth about that same time. Got a couple of dozen to Venus, which is normal. And five to Earth."

"Also probably normal."

"Yeah." Rex nodded. "But one went to the African continent, equatorial approach and three went to Ayers Landing."

"Stinking Venusians." Sykes said. Of all the Humans in the Solar System, only the Venusians were able to tolerate Earth's gravity for extended periods of time since Venus' gravity was 91% of Earth's. "They're going to take over the planet."

"They've got a pretty good start on it; Ayers Landing has two-thousand people living there. And they're starting another colony across the Gulf of Carpentaria on the other tip of land. They'll control the entire bay, Sam. Soon they'll have the entire continent as well as the islands to the north. Once they outbreed Martians, they'll be running the show. And they've got the space on Earth to do it. I'll retire to Io when that happens."

"Yeah, great. Thanks for the geography lesson. So that's where they went Ayer's Landing?" Sykes scowled; he was well aware of the Venusian's plan for Earth but there really was nothing he could do about it. "So he really is an Earthling with Venusian genetic tech. That makes sense. I'll have a word with the Governor of Venus and get to the bottom of…"

"I thought that at first as well." Rex interrupted. "But."

"But?" Sykes leaned forward closer to the monitor.

"The fifth ship went into a northern trajectory heading for the area known as Alaska." Rex interrupted.

"Alaska?" Sykes' eyebrows went up. "What's there?"

"A town called Anchorage."

"So they named the ship after their home town? Idiots."

"That's my take on it as well. They named the ship after where they were from, then realized that was a stupid move so they renamed it."

"Renamed it what?"

"The *Alba Mons*." Rex replied. "So I'm grabbing a couple of folks and heading there. They shouldn't be too hard to find, I don't think."

Governor Sykes thought back to his interaction with Hugh, and his abilities. "Only two people? I'm not sure two is enough. I'd hate for you to be caught short-handed."

"I'm touched you're worried about me." Rex said.

"I'm serious, Rex. That one named Hugh is a lot more than he appears to be."

"Yeah, okay Sam; three then. I'll take Hermann, Redd, and I guess Jennigan." Rex said. "The four of us are plenty, even with a Berserker in the mix."

"I suppose."

"We're not going to be using strong language, Sam; we'll be outfitted properly. On your expense account, of course."

"Of course. Tell Jennigan not to kill either of them." Sykes warned. "I think I want them both back here alive. I want to have a word with that lunatic with the sword about my ear. Got it?"

"Don't worry; I'll keep her on a short leash." Rex said. "Get some rest, Sam. I'll be in touch later next week. With good news."

"You better be." Governor Sykes warned then he switched off the transmission.

The End

Made in the USA
Middletown, DE
01 June 2025

76243545R00138